Acclaim for A STAB IN THE DARK

Bernal wants to purify, he wants to whip with his "palo ciego," his rough-cut blindness, his piercing pen-point that refuses the cultural slippage of a new kind of Mexican. In desperation, it seems, on a mission, Bernal documents his journeys through a morphing early 20th-century intra-nation: "Angelópolis," Mexicali, and points in between. The "authentic" dissolves in "Yankee-landia," yet it is also fused in a revolution poetry of his own — multi-voiced, odd-angled, born at the intersections of borderland lingo, personas, and formats. A profound forerunner and city street-news poet of a Latinx word howl to come. Ground-breaker, research-maker, prize igniter for a time of brave new chaos.

— Juan Felipe Herrera, U.S. Poet Laureate Emeritus

A wildly energetic journalist-writer with satirical wit, a side-order of machismo, and a lifelong distrust of politicians, Facundo Bernal might be compared to Ambrose Bierce, author of *The Devil's Dictionary*, who disappeared into Mexico during the very revolution that forced the younger Bernal north across the border. Bernal may not be a great poetic innovator, but he is a brilliant documentary versifier whose small body of work takes on a whole new life in Seidman's fabulously resuscitative translations. Bernal delivers the sounds and images of a critical epoch when a large number of Mexicans were making new lives (and a new idiom and culture) in California. His poems are caricatures, dramatic monologues, provocations. And they are also a glorious record of theater reviews, bank foreclosures, headlines, the advent of radio, immigrant labor, and overheard talk at carnivals and in dance halls. Bernal has a keen ear for the

the very alive, vernacular voice of that moment, when the City of Angels was begrudgingly adjusting to its immigrant-ushered reinvention.

— Forrest Gander, poet and translator, author of
Core Samples from the World

¡Újule! Míster Blind still sweeps the world with his "palo de ciego," his blindman's cane. Facundo Bernal's verbal theatrics, his biting insights, his astringent and truthful voice, his irreverent humor, and his great love of who he is — a Mexicano in a time when being one is both a challenge and a joy — cover as much ground today as they did in the 1920s. Then is Now: immigration, displacement, racism, the hatred of the refugee, the power of the rich, the voiceless poor, "los bichis del gud taim." ¡Cheeses Cries¡ Yankee-landia will never be the same. We needed Facundo Bernal more than ever.

— Denise Chávez, Fronteriza writer, author of
The King and Queen of Comezón

Contributors

Facundo Bernal was a poet and journalist. He was born in 1883 in Hermosillo, Mexico. He and his brother Francisco were members of the vibrant bohemian Mexican literary community of the first decades of the 20th century. He died in 1962, in Mexicali.

Anthony Seidman is the author of three collections of poetry, including *Where Thirsts Intersect* (The Bitter Oleander, 2006) and, most recently, *A Sleepless Man Sits Up in Bed* (Eyewear, 2016). He lives in Los Angeles.

Yxta Maya Murray is a novelist, art critic, and Professor of Law at Loyola Law School, Los Angeles. She writes widely on gender justice, performance art, and the intersections of law and literature.

Josh Kun is an American author, academic, music critic, and a 2016 MacArthur Fellow. He is an Associate Professor of Communication in the Annenberg School at USC and holds a joint appointment at the Department of American Studies and Ethnicity.

Gabriel Trujillo Muñoz is a poet, narrator, essayist, and professor at the Autonomous University of Baja California, Mexicali. He is widely considered one of the most important voices in contemporary Mexican science fiction.

Boris Dralyuk is the Executive Editor of the *Los Angeles Review of Books* and a literary translator.

PALOS DE CIEGO

A STAB IN THE DARK

FACUNDO BERNAL

Translated by Anthony Seidman

Foreword by Yxta Maya Murray

Introductions by Josh Kun *and* Gabriel Trujillo Muñoz

Edited by Boris Dralyuk

This is a LARB Classics publication
Published by The Los Angeles Review of Books
6671 Sunset Blvd., Suite 1521, Los Angeles, CA 90028
www.larbbooks.org

Translated poems copyright © 2018 by Anthony Seidman
Foreword copyright © 2018 by Yxta Maya Murray
Introduction copyright © 2018 by Josh Kun
Introduction copyright © 2018 by Gabriel Trujillo Muñoz
All rights reserved.

ISBN 978-1-940660-39-4

Library of Congress Cataloging-in-Publication Data
has been applied for.

Contents

Translator's Foreword

IN *PALOS DE CIEGO* Facundo Bernal employed a variety of rhyme schemes and meters typical of popular verse and of Latin American *Modernismo*. At the time, this prosody was rapidly becoming passé, yet Bernal used it with great dexterity. The macaronic rhymes and the insertion of popular *dichos* (sayings) make for a rich impasto, but the main aesthetic shock comes from Bernal's use of Mexican slang. The result is a thrilling clash of popular and lofty literary registers, English, and words that would eventually become part of the border's argot, Caló.

Several difficult decisions had to be made in order to provide an English version of *Palos de ciego* that would best guide the reader through Bernal's rollicking depiction of the borderlands. If I were to recreate the prosody exactly, the poems would sound like doggerel. Employing the meter of the English ballad would produce an anachronistic cultural mishmash. I flirted with the idea of using Blues-like structures for some of the poems. Out of despair, I even contemplated resorting to prose-block paragraphs for absolute fidelity to the text...

After deliberation, I decided that the best way to recreate this book as oral poetry was to echo the *Caló*, the slang, and the overall exuberant and spunky tone of the original, abandoning rhyme. Wherever possible, I relied on alliteration for comical effects, and I inserted contemporary American slang when appropriate. The art of "poesía para declamar" hasn't passed from the school halls and bars of Latin America; I worked to create poems that were fun to read aloud while remaining acceptably accurate. I aimed for line breaks and line lengths that were a compromise between Bernal's original Spanish and the contemporary America poetic mode, post-William Carlos Williams, Robert Creeley, et al. My priority was to preserve the popular speech. Indeed, words like "bichi" (Northern Mexican Spanish for "naked," derived from the English word "beach") pepper the text, as do idioms — for example, the collection's title. "*Dar palos de ciego*" (literally, "to thrash with the stick of a blind man") implies to struggle vainly, clutching at straws, but also alludes to the blind man's cane and to Míster Blind, who appears as one of the characters. Many thanks to Boris Dralyuk, who suggested *A Stab in the Dark* as a reasonable transformation of the Spanish title into English. I then incorporated this titular motif into the poems wherever there is mention of blindness, canes, and the thrashing of canes.

This English version includes the entire text except for one delightful short poem titled "Eche usted nombre de frutas," which relies entirely on puns. It lists fruits, many of which don't have a proper name in English, and are known by loan words such as "*mamey*." The Spanish text speaks for itself in the second half of the book.

It's important to note the publication year of Bernal's collection: 1923. A year prior, César Vallejo published his masterpiece *Trilce* and forever changed the Spanish poetic mode, with his pioneering use of white space, his radical new line breaks, and his neologisms. The *Creacionismo* of Vicente Huidobro was making a buzz in the literary world, and the avant-garde poet Kyn Taniya was taking off with his *Aeroplane*. All of those works were more transformative for Spanish literature at large, but *A Stab in the Dark* was the first collection of poetry to reflect the border, the Mexican north, the reality of *Mexicanos* in Los Angeles, and the nascence of Chicano culture, all in a Spanish that is uniquely Bernal's.

I first discovered Bernal's poetry on the bookshelves of my wife, the *cachanilla* detective fiction writer Nylsa Martínez — mostly in Gabriel Trujillo Muñoz's anthologies and essays on

Baja California literature. I owe her many thanks for helping me understand the more difficult passages, as I made my stabs in the dark. Thanks also to the poet and critic Martín Camps, who helped me on other passages, and for his years of friendship. Thanks to Gabriel Trujillo Muñoz for providing us access to the works of Facundo Bernal, as well as for his enthusiasm with regards to the project. And very deep gratitude to Boris Dralyuk, for thinking of me when planning this project.

As always, my guide in translation is Paul Blackburn, whose *Poem of the Cid* has been my beacon for many years. I will lift his words for this book: *Please enjoy it, and remember, read it aloud.*

Anthony Seidman
San Fernando Valley
2018

"For the *Raza*, for the Homeland, and for Art"

Yxta Maya Murray

WITH HIS GROUCHY, thrumming poems, Facundo Bernal reminds us that "assimilation" is a myth. Writing in the 1920s while living between Los Angeles and Mexicali, the Sonoran-born Bernal complains relentlessly, and often hilariously, about how bad it is "here" and how great it is "back home." In so doing, he records the early days of a century-long Latinx resistance and adaptation to the exhausting, grotesque, and often boring dynamics of colonialism.

L.A., the land of film stars and millionaires, is violent, he bemoans in "The Crime Wave." For Bernal, the city is no new Xanadu that offers a fresh start from the traumas of the 1910 Revolution. Its distracting scenic beauty only masks horrible dangers: while the city has "parks brimming with lush lakesides" and "is covered/ by a cloak of fog/ as white as a bull's eye," it is also teeming with Charles Manson-like villains *avant la lettre*: "and now the victim's a lady/ shot dead by some punks/ for no clear motive,/ but according/ to their statement,/ they were instructed by Spirit X/ or perhaps the Devil himself."

Bernal struggles to understand how the Latinos who have moved to L.A. in the hopes of a better life can not only stand it in this strange city, but adapt its mores to their own. In *"Pochos"* (the name of this poem, of course, referring to the old insult to Anglo-acting Mexican-Americans), he "focus[es] on/ those from back home/ who land here, observe things,/ and never imitate what's good,/ but only what's terrible." "What's terrible'" is affecting the "gringo" habits of gum-chewing and tobacco-spitting, not to mention a man's parading his half-dressed Chicana girlfriend around town: her "angelic face/ (and I use that adjective in quotes)/ has been buried beneath/ makeup and rouge;/ her skirt/ allows me to glimpse/ the exact position of her garters,/ which move farther and farther,/ like 'seabirds (sorry to wax/ poetic!) in steady flight.'"

In "Raking up the Past," Bernal continues this screed by "dedicat[ing] a few 'stabs'/ to the people of my *Raza*/ who leave Mexico, and when they've/ barely set foot in Yankee-landia,/ forget their Spanish/ and disown their Homeland." The most alarming of these *Raza* are the women "who wear extra-short skirts,/ and dance the 'Hula-Hula,'" only to then "express themselves/ in the language of Byron,/ because they no *hablan* 'Spanish.'"

As this recitation demonstrates, Bernal often exorcises his angry nostalgia on misbehaving women, who buy into a deracinated U.S. culture that is agog with technology and parlous to love and family. In "The Radio," he offers the tale of a wayward wife who would rather listen to her favorite singer than cook her husband dinner: "'Woman,/ it's already eight o'clock,/ and I haven't had a bite to eat / .../ and instead of cooking me/ some supper — dammit! —/ you're listening to gossip,/ to music and jingles!" "Quiet!" the wife hisses. "Don't make noise,/ Lázaro is singing..."

But even within Bernal's colorful complaints about distaff cultural disobedience, he also sketches portraits of Mexican-American women who aren't so much assimilating to the decadence of U.S. society as busting out on their own. If they're not wearing visible garters, dancing the hula, or dreaming in their kitchens, he explains mock-seriously in "A Sermon," then they are "swimming in public places,/ where modesty is shipwrecked/ while sin sails forth."

Actually, Bernal insinuates, he'd like to dip a toe into that pool himself — except that it's deadly dull in the U.S., with its false piety, typified by laws prohibiting the sale of alcohol on Sundays. Though the California Supreme Court struck down the state's blue law in 1858, repressive customs hung on into the 1920s. As Bernal laments in "Blue Sunday": "If anyone's eyes/ should focus/ on certain ladies'/ curves, they're guilty/ (for that's the age-/ old law), and that gaze/ will be fined/ 20 smackeroos."

Still, when seeking consolation, Bernal knows where to go. He exits from the confusions and corruptions of Californian modernity and returns to his macho roots. In "The Bullfight," he recounts a spectacle in Mexicali. Here, the toreador "flutters his cape, regaling us/ with the best of the best./ The enemy is enshrouded/ in the folds of the cape, and Torquito caresses/ his horns. Reveilles shower down upon him/ as he walks through the flower-fall,/ among trumpet blasts, shouts, ovations..."

Sometimes perfection can surface even in L.A., during those rare moments of grace when "home" and "here" can co-exist without harming each other. In *A Stab in the Dark's* final poem, "*México Auténtico*," Bernal recounts a concert in the now-defunct Philharmonic Auditorium. In July 1923, this venue hosted the radiant Nelly Fernández and her all-Mexican troupe of singers and dancers. Bernal was enchanted by the indigenous performers, who brought to Southern California all of the magic it ordinarily lacked. On that charmed evening, "Four little Mexican women/ dancing gracefully ... small of foot, vast of soul,/ eyes black as obsidian,/ and lips like coral [made] up the chorus:/ almost a choir of angels..." Like Bernal in these poems, the performers worked "their hearts out '*For the* Raza,/ *for the Homeland, and for Art.*"

"Defending What's Rightly Ours":
An Introduction to Facundo Bernal's
Forgotten Masterpiece of
Los Angeles Literature

Josh Kun

IN 1923, a syndicate of African-American investors from Los Angeles and a team of mayors and local civic and business leaders in Northern Mexico decided that Baja California needed a "Negro Sanitarium." The proposed health spa was a tourist pitch under the banner of interracial brotherhood, and it required cross-border buy-in.

In Los Angeles, Charlotta Bass, the publisher of the pioneering African-American newspaper *The California Eagle*, did her part to fundraise, as did Agustín Haro y Tamariz, editor of *La Prensa*, the city's first Spanish-language weekly. The Louisiana jazz legend Kid Ory, summering in Los Angeles, played a benefit show in Exposition Park. And down at the border in Calexico, the poet and journalist Facundo Bernal hustled donations at a rate of 50 cents for each brick in the sanitarium's walls; he had been living in the growing border community since leaving Los Angeles five years earlier.[1] Bernal was originally from Sonora,

---

1   For more on this campaign, see Ted Vincent, "Black Hopes in Baja California: Black American and Mexican Cooperation, 1917-1926," *Western Journal of Black Studies* 21, no. 3 (Fall 1997), pp. 204-213. For a larger view of relations between Black Los Angeles and Baja California, see Josh Kun, "Tijuana and the Borders of Race," in *A Companion to Los Angeles*, edited by William Deverell and Greg Hise (Malden, MA: Wiley-Blackwell, 2010), pp. 313-26.

but by 1923 he had become a key figure in Southern California-Baja California life and letters and a member of a bilingual and multicultural network of writers, artists, entrepreneurs, and politicians who took L.A.'s ties to Mexico seriously. The volume you hold in your hands, *Palos de Ciego* — his first and only book — was published in Los Angeles that same year. It consists of poems that originally ran in the pages of *La Prensa*, poems that, like Bernal himself, moved back and forth between the cultural and political worlds of Los Angeles and Northern Mexico. It was a time, before fences, walls, and the Border Patrol, when the border only existed to be crossed.

Bernal first crossed it in 1913, on his way to East Los Angeles. As an outspoken journalist in his hometown of Hermosillo, Bernal was a relentless critic of local politicians struggling for power in the thick of the Mexican Revolution. He received a number of death threats and, after one stint in jail, was promised a lifetime of imprisonment if he didn't leave the country. He came to L.A. on the run, a journalist in exile, and his byline soon appeared in the *Los Angeles Times* (attached to a feature on the revolution in Sonora[2]) and on the pages of some of the city's most important Spanish-language periodicals: *El Heraldo de México*, *El Eco de Mexico*, and *La Prensa*. Writing didn't pay all the bills, so after a brief stint in a factory packing tomatoes, he also began working at his brother's clothing store, Casa Bernal Hermanos, selling bespoke suits. Bernal spent four years in the city, immersing himself in its thriving and rapidly expanding community of Mexican immigrants; he followed local news and politics as closely as he followed developments back home in Sonora. Even when he left to open another branch of the family's business in the Mexican border town of Mexicali, Los Angeles remained central to his writing.

In 1921, Bernal began publishing a series of poems in *La Prensa* — a paper that declared itself to be "*por la patria y por la raza*" (for the Mexican nation and the Mexican race) — under the pseudonym of "Míster Blind." The paper's "new collab-

---

2 "La ultima revolución en Sonora," *Los Angeles Times*, 17 August 1913: 56.

orator" and his poems "about current politics and events" were announced in a bold text box on the paper's front page. Bernal's weekly verse chronicles, which could be as satirical and smug as they were sincere and culturally flag-waving, appeared alongside advertisements for a Mexican *pastelería* on Spring Street, a funeral home on Figueroa, a Chinese herbalist on Alameda, an "American" dentist on Main Street, the Commercial National Bank on Spring, and El Progreso restaurant on Main — which offered "platillos netamente Mexicanos" (truly Mexican dishes) but was owned and run by Chinese immigrants, the Quon Chong Company.

By the time Bernal compiled his poems into a book, they had already established him as a trusted cross-border tribune and recorder, a leading authority on Mexican life both in Los Angeles and in Mexicali and Sonora. In fact, according to Mexican author and literary scholar Gabriel Trujillo Muñoz, *Palos de Ciego* was a pioneering expression of a regional identity, of "a way of life, of a merger of beliefs and customs, of a historical stage of development and consolidation of Mexico's northern border, which is to say, of border society — call it Sonoran, Chicano, or Baja Californian."[3] Or call it, for that matter, Angeleno.

WHERE DOES the literature of Los Angeles begin? *Palos de Ciego* is one of the first books of poems about the city, and yet it is nowhere to be found in accounts of L.A. literary history. Although it followed Horace Bell's *Reminiscences of a Ranger: Early Times in Southern California* (1881) — thought to be first book printed in Los Angeles — and a number of other celebrated works such as Helen Hunt Jackson's *Ramona* (1884), *Palos de Ciego* appeared years before L.A. really burst onto the literary scene in 1939, with the publication of John Fante's *Ask the Dust*, Nathanael West's *The Day of the Locust*, and Raymond Chandler's *Big Sleep*. It also just preceded works with which it had much

---

3   Gabriel Trujillo Muñoz, *Un Camino de hallazgos: poetas bajacalifornianos del siglo veinte* (Mexicali: Universidad Autónoma de Baja California, 1992, 1992), p. 15.

in common: Japanese immigrant novelist Shoson Nagahara's *Lament in the Night* (1925) and *The Tale of Osato* (1925-26) — the latter of which was, like *Palos*, originally serialized in an L.A. paper, the Japanese daily *Rafu Shimpo*; Arna Bontemps's 1931 novel of Black Los Angeles, *God Sends Sunday*; and the very first novel of Mexican-American life in Los Angeles, *Las Aventuras de Don Chipote, o Cuando los pericos mamen* (1928, translated in 2000 as *The Adventures of Don Chipote, or, When Parrots Breast-Feed*) by the Mexican journalist, playwright, and novelist Daniel Venegas.

Raised in Guadalajara, Venegas arrived in L.A. in 1924 and his novel, released by the publishing arm of *El Heraldo de México*, has long been considered the starting point of the city's Chicano literature and the first book to employ early forms of "Spanglish." *Palos de Ciego* checked the same boxes five years earlier. One explanation for the book's lack of visibility is that it barely circulated in the 1920s. A warehouse flood destroyed many of the original copies. Yet even after Trujillo Muñoz excavated it for re-publication in Baja California in 1989, *Palos* is still mostly regarded as a milestone of *poesía urbana* (urban poetry) in the literature of Northern Mexico.[4] Bernal's significance extends far north of the border as well. He is one of transnational border modernism's greatest literary interpreters.

During the period chronicled in Palos, the greater U.S.-Mexico borderland was in the midst of a modernizing boom.[5] Beyond

---

4 Trujillo Muñoz has anthologized Bernal in the canon of Baja California literature. See, for example, *Entrecruzamientos. La cultura baja-californiana, sus autores y sus obras* (México: Universidad Autónoma de Baja California, 2002); *Mensajeros de Heliconia. Capítulos sueltos de las letras bajacalifornianas 1832-2004* (México: Universidad Autónoma de Baja California, 2004); and *La cultura bajacaliforniana y otros ensayos afines* (Mexico: Consejo Nacional para la Cultura y las Artes, 2005).

5 For more on various approaches to border and migrant modernism, see Christopher Schedler, *Border Modernism: Intercultural Readings in American Literary Modernism* (New York: Routledge, 2002); Ramón Saldívar, *The Borderlands of Culture: Américo Paredes and the Transnational Imaginary* (Durham, N.C.: Duke University

the growth of U.S. railroad and mining industries, border tourism was on the rise and the first border radio stations were broadcasting north and south of the line. A community of artists, writers, journalists, and musicians were seeking to make sense of a cross-border ecology and culture that were still less than half a century old, and Bernal was an important voice in that effort. The fact that Palos was published in Los Angeles, and that its cross-border content begins and ends in L.A., testifies to the city's direct connection to the history of transnational border modernism. Unfortunately, that connection has been largely lost in tellings of L.A. literary history. In a recent re-evaluation of the Latinx roots of L.A. literature, Victor Valle takes literary historians and anthologists to task for turning Latinx non-fiction writers into literary ghosts: "The [L.A.] canon's lingering reluctance to account for narratives that deliberately undermine or ignore the fixities of national borders thus ensures the invisibility of the serpentine routes through which Latina/o non-fiction writers invent their urban 'native' identities."[6] The same could be said for generically challenging works like *Palos de Ciego*, which blend non-fiction with fiction, poetry with journalism, etc. — works that define their own forms of "radical cosmopolitanism" rooted in the migrant, cross-border experiences of early 20th-century Los Angeles.

Press, 2006); Alicia Schmidt Camacho, *Migrant Imaginaries: Latino Cultural Politics in the U.S.-Mexico Borderlands* (New York: New York University Press, 2008); Rachel Adams, *Continental Divides: Remapping the Cultures of North America* (Chicago: University of Chicago Press, 2009); and José David Saldívar, *Trans-Americanity: Subaltern Modernities, Global Coloniality, and the Cultures of Greater Mexico* (Durham, N.C.: Duke University Press, 2012).
6   Victor Valle, "LA's Latina/o Phantom Nonfiction and the Technologies of Literary Secrecy," in *Latinx Writing Los Angeles: Nonfiction Dispatches from a Decolonial Rebellion*, edited by Ignacio López-Calvo and Victor Valle (Lincoln: University of Nebraska Press, 2018), p. 7.

THE LOS ANGELES sections of *Palos de Ciego* give us a detailed, vibrant account of a city in the midst of an immigrant transformation. Between 1910 and 1930, close to a million Mexican immigrants fled the political upheavals of the Mexican Revolution and settled in the U.S., seeking freedom and work in the booming industries of the Southwest. Los Angeles, which was rapidly expanding its industrial base and fast becoming a capital of leisure and entertainment, was the most popular destination. In 1920, the Mexican population of Los Angeles reached 30,000; by 1930, it more than tripled. Among the Mexican newcomers was "an entrepreneurial class of refugees," as Nicolás Kanellos has written, who were instrumental in shaping a circle of industries — journalism, entertainment, and commerce — that actively promoted the interests of "México de afuera" (Mexico beyond Mexico).[7] The paper in which *Palos de Ciego* first appeared, *La Prensa*, was just one of a series of influential but short-lived Spanish-language newspapers that had been covering Mexican Los Angeles since 1851. There had already been *La Estrella de Los Ángeles*, *El Clamor Público*, and *La Crónica*, and when Bernal was writing as "Míster Blind," *La Gaceta de los Estados Unidos* (founded in 1917) and *El Heraldo de México* (founded in 1915) were covering similar beats — beats that, in 1926, would be taken over by *La Opinión*, still the largest Spanish-language paper in the country.

Bernal's Los Angeles poems — written at the end of the Mexican Revolution and at the start of Prohibition — were mostly inspired by and addressed to the city's growing Mexican population, fellow "foreigners / living in Yankee-landia." His lines are

7 Nicolás Kanellos, "A Brief History of Hispanic Periodicals in the United States," in Hispanic Periodicals in the United States, Origins to 1960: A Brief History and Comprehensive Bibliography, edited by Nicolás Kanellos and Helvetia Martell (Houston: Arte Público Press, 2000), p. 32. See also Ramón D. Chacón, "The Chicano Immigrant Press in Los Angeles: The Case of 'El Heraldo de México,' 1916-1920," *Journalism History* 4, no. 2 (Summer 1977), pp. 48-50, 62-64.

populated by Mexican politicians, generals, and actors, by labor unions and corrupt landlords. *Palos* occupies multiple geographies at once — Los Angeles, Mexicali, Sonora — and Bernal explores just how much each place influences the others. He shows, for instance, how the Volstead Act's drying up of California (and wetting up of Baja) impacted border tourist economies and U.S. stereotypes of Mexican culture. He imagines a "Letter Sent from Mexico to Los Angeles, Calif." and a "Letter Sent from Los Angeles to Mexico." In the former, a man in Jauja, Michoacán, learns about his L.A. bank going bankrupt by reading *La Prensa*; in the latter, his *compadre* reveals that his heart breaks with longing for Mexico. He is stuck in Los Angeles, "lurching in place."

Bernal's L.A. poems move across the city, riding streetcars to Venice Beach and other seaside resorts and dancehalls, but also up and down Broadway, Main, New High, and Alameda, the downtown avenues of Mexican business and culture, which were home to many film and vaudeville (or *variedades*) theaters, whose productions also find their way into his verse.[8] He writes about the sunshine of "the beautiful Angelo-polis," but also of its violent noir — including a "crimson wave of crime" against women that leaves a "gruesome tableau" in its wake: "dirty chunks" of flesh "slicked with blood,/ and splattered/ with brain matter."

Bernal also castigates "Bad Mexicans," who've assimilated too quickly the mores of Yankee-landia, and in so doing anticipates Octavio Paz's now infamous critique of Mexicans in Los Angeles as orphans stuck in limbo between cultures and languages.[9] Like Paz, Bernal sees the city's potential to diminish Mexican identity and encourage the rise of the *pocho*, a deorgatory term for Mexicans in the U.S who are seen to have abandoned their na-

8   For an excellent overview of this entertainment industry, see Colin Gunckel, *Mexico on Main Street: Transnational Film Culture in Los Angeles Before World War II* (Rutgers, N.J.: Rutgers University Press, 2015).

9   Octavio Paz, "The Pachuco and Other Extremes," in *The Labyrinth of Solitude*, translated by Lysander Kemp (New York: Grove Press, 1961), pp. 9-28.

tive culture. In "Raking up the Past," he dedicates "a few 'stabs'/ to the people of my *Raza*/ who leave Mexico, and when they've/ barely set foot in Yankee-landia,/ forget their Spanish/ and disown their Homeland." He is particularly hard on Mexican women who he believes have fallen from grace under the spell of L.A.'s charms, donning short skirts, dancing the hula, chewing gum, and speaking only "in the language of Byron." He takes more stabs in "*Pochos*," targeting "those from back home/ who land here, observe things,/ and never imitate what's good,/ but only what's terrible." He berates their bilingualisms but, ironically, does a great service by committing to the page some of the very first instances of Spanglish in Los Angeles writing: "*sun-ah-va-gún*," "*What su mara?*," "*gud taim*," and "*Cheeses Cries.*" And so he becomes, despite himself, the forerunner of El Piporro, Cheech & Chong, Guillermo Gómez-Peña, and Don Cheto.

Bernal's excoriations of Gringofied Mexicans were part of a larger battle to defend Mexican culture and Mexican people in "México de afuera" generally, and in the often especially hostile spaces of Southern California specifically. The first poem in the book aligns Bernal's own exilic patriotism with that of *La Prensa* itself, lauding the paper's pages for exuding "*Mexicanismo*" and always supporting "THE HOMELAND AND ITS PEOPLE!" Bernal was just one of many Mexican journalists, publishers, business owners, and civic leaders in the Los Angeles outpost working to invent, support, and market an authentic and uniform vision of conservative Mexican identity. His poems were consistently "on message" with the reporting and editorials of *La Prensa* and *El Heraldo*: don't be tempted by Yankee-landia — stay Catholic, stay moral, and speak Spanish.[10]

Although he is critical of "Bad Mexicans," Bernal's allegiance to his homeland and his people mostly takes the form of protest

---

10   This trend has been well documented by many scholars. See, for example, Kanellos, "A Brief History of Hispanic Periodicals in the United States"; George J. Sanchez, *Becoming Mexican American: Ethnicity, Culture, and Identity in Chicano Los Angeles, 1900-1945* (Oxford: Oxford University Press, 1993); and Colin Gunckel, *Mexico on Main Street.*

poems "defending what's rightly ours" and railing against injustices suffered by immigrants. In "Raking Up The Past," he lifts his lance (as he puts it) against "Jewish grifters and/ wholesale jewelry merchants," shady employment agencies and professional lodges, and anyone else with plans to "exploit our *Raza*." Up and down the Mexican main drag in "Short Films," Bernal meets only a rogue's gallery of "merciless" anti-Mexican "swindlers:" lying tailors, wily watch salesmen, and deceitful haberdashers.

He dedicates one poem, "Let's Save Our Brother from the Hangman," to Aureliano (Aurelio) Pompa, an immigrant laborer from Bernal's home state in Sonora, who came to Los Angeles "seeking work in/ this Babylon," his head full of "pipe dreams." What Pompa receives instead is constant physical abuse and harassment from his Anglo carpenter foreman. After shooting the foreman in self-defense, Pompa is arrested, tried, and sentenced to execution. Bernal uses his poem to raise funds and try to prevent the hanging: "LET US ALL HELP/ AURELIANO POMPA." But the effort is in vain. Besides finding its way into Bernal's poem, Pompa's story became the plot of one of the very first commercially recorded corridos (Mexican border ballads) in the United States. Set in Los Angeles and recorded in New York in 1924, "Vida, Proceso, y Muerte de Aurelio Pompa" ("The Life, Trial, and Death of Aurelio Pompa") was subsequently sold as a phonographic disc to Mexican laborers across the United States. "Tell my race not to come here," the song went. "For here they will suffer/ There is no pity here."

That suffering, that lack of pity, is one of the great themes of this collection. In one poem, "Mexico in Caricature," Bernal reviews a play staged at a theater on Broadway that portrayed the border crossing from Mexicali into Calexico, a crossing that, by 1923, the poet knew all too well. Bernal was outraged by the play's depictions of Mexicans as sombrero-wearing and rifle-toting bandits: "If I could have set off/ an explosion, both playwright/ and protagonist would have/ been blown to smithereens." He calls for a boycott of the theater for "denigrat[ing] what is ours" and darkening "honor of a free people/ deserving all due respect/ from the largest, most cultured/ country in the Universe."

Palos de Ciego ends on a more proactive and laudatory note. After a series of poems about Mexicali (baseball! heat!), Bernal returns to downtown Los Angeles for a June 1923 performance of a variety show titled "*Mexico Auténtico*." The show ran for three weeks and featured an all-star lineup of singers and dancers from Mexico City's national theater, including character actor Ernesto Finance, dancer Rafael Diaz, opera singer Isabel Zenteno (Bernal liked how she "makes us feel, to our cores,/ the national ballads"), and singer and dancer Nelly Fernández ("Nelly, graceful Nelly"). The review of the show in the *Los Angeles Times* focused on the auditorium's empty seats ("the Mexican colony, even, is not turning out as it should"), but Bernal only saw a full-house success — a proud representation of a proud people in which his readers, in turn, should take pride. "Let these poor lines go forth," he writes in the closing poem of his book, "as a humble homage,/ full of love and admiration/ for the great artists who work/ their hearts out 'For the Raza,/ for the Homeland, and for Art.'" This, Bernal insists, is how Mexican Los Angeles should look and how it should be understood. This is how culture ought to flow back and forth across borders. This is what Los Angeles should admire.

Facundo Bernal López (1883-1962)

Gabriel Trujillo Muñoz

FACUNDO BERNAL is a man from the North. A son of Sonora, he was forced to leave his native state, and even his country, in order to escape political violence and upheaval. But Don Facundo, as his colleagues in the press would call him, was always a Sonoran at heart. He was born on October 16, 1883, in Hermosillo, the first son of Facundo Bernal Sr. and Luisa López de Bernal. His father worked for the state government, and the family's economic situation was precarious, like that of many in Sonora in the years before the Revolution. Facundo Jr. received a secular fourth grade education from the Colegio Sonora, a public school. After the early death of Facundo Sr., the son took a government post no less dreary and miserable that the one his father had occupied. Yet he continued to educate himself with the help of his cultured mother, who ensured that no matter how difficult life was at the Bernal household, there was never a lack of books. Facundo read the poets of the Golden Age of Spanish literature — Garcilaso de la Vega, Francisco de Quevedo, Luis de Góngora, and Lope de Vega — as well as the Romantics and the Latin American *Modernistas*, especially Rubén Darío, Gutiérrez Nájera, and Amado Nervo. This bookishness was not uncommon in Hermosillo, which was home to small but busy communities of foreign-born residents — French, North American, and English — brought to the region by the politic ups and downs of Maximilian's empire, as well as Don Porfirio Díaz's campaign for foreign investment. The town was close to the port of Guaymas, and was a stop on the new railroad, which brought not only raw materials, but also books, newspapers, and magazines from the interior of the country and from abroad.

This all contributed to a vibrant cultural atmosphere. Presiding over it were Manuel Campillo and Rodolfo Campodonico (1866-1926), who were troubadours of popular verse rather than champions of Latin American *Modernismo*, and clearly influenced Facundo's poetic sensibility. And there was never a lack of political disputes in the town, nor a shortage of literary salons, dances, and bohemian gatherings replete with musicians and poets improvising, *mano a mano*, songs and poems celebrating their respective sweethearts. It's no surprise, then, that Facundo — like his younger brother Francisco, born on October 4, 1896 — formed closer friendships with troubadours and musicians like Chito Peralta and Campodonico than they did with writers. Culture back then meant political rallies, dances, and block parties. Naturally, it found written expression most readily in journalism.

Facundo soon became an important voice in the Sonoran press, which itself became a prime mover behind the Revolution. He published teasingly erotic romantic sonnets along with articles and sarcastic verses targeting the arbitrary decisions of politicians and the greed of the mercantile class. It's important to note that, in Sonoran society in those days, a writer was no better than any of the other locals, serving as something like a social worker, a promoter of interpersonal relationships, and an unofficial spokesperson for the community. Facundo's writing possessed social utility, and had direct economic benefits for him personally. Consider this early poem, a parody of Manuel Acuña's suicidal "Nocturno a Rosario," which Facundo wrote to protest a promotion to Manager-Collector granted to the Copyist-Correspondent of Sonora's General Treasury Office:

> So. I must
> inform the treasurer,
> inform him that my

sad situation overwhelms me,
for I have been only
a Manager-Collector
for three whole years;
so profoundly do I suffer,
so profoundly do I wait
for them to regale me
with a pen set, and not a broom.

I would beg that they recall
how many years past
I did request the post
which today I learned was filled;
let them know
these hopes of mine
have been dashed;
and my joys have been drained
because of that yearned-for post;
let them know
that from my precipice
the future blackens deeply.
At night, when I ponder,
(with my soul thrashing),
how others so easily do find
their station rising,
and their wages plentiful,
yet they work hardly at all,
it does spur me to ponder matters,
and in the end, my luck depleted,
I recall that another day
slaving behind the broom awaits me.

I grasp how that job
never shall be mine,
never shall I earn
those 80 pesos;
however, I do persist,

and in promotions I believe;
today cruel fate
may show me his black shoulder,
yet instead of being less trustful,
I am all the more hopeful.
At times I think of flinging
my eternal "I quit"
in the faces of the cursed
feather duster and perfidious broom!
And yet if all is in vain,
if I have no exit hence,
if the bill collectors
finish me off,
what else do they ask
that I do in such a circumstance?

Here we see an account of Facundo's economic situation, which was that of all of his family, as well as the majority of the incipient middle class in Sonora. That class got by on stoic hope — a feature of Northern Mexico's Protestant-like ethic, which insisted that hard work would eventually lead to material results. This poem bears proof of Facundo's poetic skill and sense of humor, his empathy for his fellow citizens, and his tendency to use — and ironize — his own life experiences as subject matter. Thanks to this poem, Facundo obtained his own promotion:

And I who so attempted
to earn a decent wage,
then sport a good suit
and lavish gifts on my sweetheart,
even just by saving what "Smith" charges
for fees, well... I could
pay what's needed to those
necessary, despite a month
of being unemployed...
How sweet it would be
to live while preying

on a juicier paycheck;
The English pleased,
I, always, satisfied,
without seeking their bosses,
saying, in spite,
I have only a few days left,
for the love of the God.
Just realize how exquisite
these brief hours of life prove,
how beautiful proves existence
with a job like that,
and I dreamed of such
"oh, deceitful fate," and,
while maddened, I would think
(my soul trembling),
I would think of making myself old,
here, just for now.

Lord knows
that was my most splendid dream,
my glowing hope,
my bliss and pleasure;
God well knows it was not in vain
that I pinned my efforts
(I say this although they
smash my soul with a log)
on how to live bare-bones
just like I did yesterday.
That was my hope...
Oh, Seductive Open Positions,
scant help
exists between you two;
Adieu
My Benefactors,
Feather Duster and Shower Stall, and My Broom: Adieu.

Facundo's readiness to address the social life of his community — principally that of Hermosillo — is also characteristic of his poetry. His poems do not keep a safe distance from popular culture; instead, they are almanacs of that culture. Within them, one encounters scandalous gossip, prejudices, and the major and minor struggles of the population residing in northern Mexico. Facundo's poetry functions as a chronicle documenting the social transformations of his time, written from the perspective of a fellow citizen who relies on humor as a defense against disaster and injustice.

A poem like the "Ice Skaters," written in 1912, perfectly captures Facundo's capacity to blend genuine sentiment with irony. It recounts events that would regularly take place on Sundays in the corridors of the Colegio Sonora, where young couples would gather to ice skate and dance. The piece reads like a less heroic version of Rubén Darío's "Marcha triunfal" (1905), yet it brims with the same optimism and joy at the sight of a young northern woman dancing:

> With their hickish squires
> the Queens of the Fiesta
> parade down the corridors...
> The chords of the orchestra resound
> as they embark on the sweetest and slowest waltz;
> they come to the dance; and to me
> they seem to be exquisite pullets,
> fresh rose petals shivering,
> ruffled by the wind.
> The squires swirl
> while dancing
> and utter amorous phrases,
> glistening things
> like set jewels,
> diamonds and sapphires;
> and their gazes are enveloped
> in the honey of sighs,
> and in the light of hope.

While a couple passes by me,
a voice reaches my ear,
an aching voice
moaning about
absence and oblivion.

Sweet Argentine voices,
fresh laughter of sopranos;
a stirring of colors
in the silk of skirt and bodice;
and a tear that rolls
down the snow-and-rose-colored mien
of a gorgeous damsel
who has buried her love.

When the Revolution of Francisco I. Madero (1873-1913) brought an end to the reign of the dictator Don Porfirio Díaz (1830-1915) in 1910, dances and ice skating became things of the past for most Mexicans, but life in Sonora remained more or less unchanged until 1913. Still, the more progressive sectors of Sonoran society viewed Madero's government, though not Madero himself, as less revolutionary then they had hoped for, and friendlier to those who still supported Porfirio Díaz than to those who had fought for a democratic regime. That disillusionment was further increased by the Orozco rebellion, which erupted in Chihuahua and reached Sonora by the middle of 1912 as the war against the Yaquis — the cause of, or excuse for, countless atrocities. Add to that the serious problems plaguing the regime of José María Maytorena (1867-1948), then Governor of Sonora, with various municipalities seeking ever greater autonomy.

At the age of 30, Facundo Bernal was one of the most combative journalists in Mexico. He published his own newspaper, *Rey Momo,* a name taken from the character in carnivals who represented happiness and festivity. It was in this newspaper that, in 1913, Facundo baptized Rosendo Rosado, then Secretary of the Sonoran Government, as "Cat with Neck," a nickname that would hound the politico until the end of his life, and which may have brought about Facundo's forced exile. By the end of 1912, as a result of his writings against Maytorena, he was a lodger in the notorious prison of Sonora. A photograph from January 1913 depicts Facundo among other political prisoners and guards. This photograph shows a group of dashing gentlemen, in a state of perfect health, gathered together for some civilized purpose. The truth, of course, was quite different. An attempt was made on Facundo's life by the prison guards. He only avoided death because one of the guards, who held his verse in high esteem, gave him advance warning. Facundo's daughter, Angelina Bernal, tells the story:

> Even while in jail, he continued to write articles against the government. His own mother, Doña Luisa López, would take them out from beneath the dirty dishes in the basket in which she used to deliver his meals. That's why they decided to kill him, because even though he was imprisoned, they couldn't quiet him. But one of the guards advised him of their plans. He told him that they were going to shoot him from a position on the roof. Facundo moved the cot on which he slept to another side of the cell. And that night, just like the guard said, someone fired some rounds at the spot where he usually slept.

By February 1913, the political situation in Mexico was on the verge of disaster; a decade of tragedies, the assassinations of Madero and his Vice President, José María Pino Suárez (1869-1913), the regime of Victoriano Huerta (1850-1916) and his stuffed shirts, the armed insurrection in Coahuila led by Venustiano Carranza (1859-1920), and, just a short while later, a direct confrontation between the main political figures presiding over Sonora. Moderates begged for armed help and power against the Huerta uprising. Indignation brimmed over in every "pueblo" and "ranchería." The Sonorans, who never resisted in using their own weapons, blocked road crossings, occupied government buildings, and claimed public and private properties as their own. Faced with chaos, Maytorena asked for a license from the local congress, but the congress instead named Ignacio L. Persqueira as Governor on February 25. A few days later, during the first days of March, Facundo left the Sonora prison — not to live in freedom, but to leave the state at once, under threat of further imprisonment if he were apprehended. For Facundo, abandoning his beloved Hermosillo was immensely painful. But there was no other option. And the only road to freedom led him north, far from the great battles and privations of the Mexican Revolution.

One of Facundo's brothers, Pedro, was already living in Los Angeles, California, and so the Bernal family could count on stable, if crowded, living quarters. Neither Facundo's mother nor his other siblings — Ricardo, Francisco, Enriqueta, and Carmelita — wished to remain in Hermosillo. If Facundo were to set off, so would the entire Bernal clan. This hasty departure was traumatic for all of them. Half a century later, Fransciso described how that radical change altered their lives forever: "School had recently been cancelled, and then unforeseen political circumstances prevented me from taking advantage of a scholarship and continuing my studies at the university in Mexico City, as had some of my high school companions, like Juan de Dios Bojórquez and Francisco Terminel, who both found work in the government; the first one became the General Secretary and the second one led the cabinet for agriculture under Plutarco Elías Calles."[11] The destiny awaiting Facundo and Francisco would be less powerful, but more humane. In March 1913 the Bernals took the road towards the city of Los Angeles, which was by then already the playground of gangsters and dazzling movie stars.

---

11   See note to "The Presidential Succession."

From Los Angeles to Mexicali

THAT SAME MARCH, after a stop in Tucson, Arizona, the Bernals reached Los Angeles. They were among the many Mexicans crossing the border each day to reach American soil. The primary motive for this was the Revolution's violence: forced conscription, firing squads, looting, and bombings. Those who had no economic means or family on "the other side" ended up in the refugee camps that the United States government set up to control the flow of immigrants. Those who could rely on funds or personal contacts had no problems reaching their destinations. Such was the luck of the Bernal family.

At the time of Facundo's and Francisco's arrival, Los Angeles confined the Mexican minority population to *barrios* located east of the Los Angeles River, despite the community's growing influence on the city's economy and social life. The Bernal family permanently settled in the house of Pedro, a humble clothing merchant. Facundo soon found employment in a tomato cannery, but he wasn't cut out for the daily grind; sensing his impending failure as a worker, he decided to help his brother with his business instead. Soon, however, he found an even more suitable occupation, becoming a stringer for the most important Spanish-language newspapers of the time, such as *El Eco de México*, *La Prensa*, and *El Heraldo de México*.

Facundo's stay in Los Angeles lasted from 1913 to 1917. As Pedro's clothing business provided more dividends, he asked his brothers to establish a similar storefront in Mexicali — a first step toward sending the entire family back to Mexico. Mexicali, which had been founded in 1903, was a perfect choice for this plan: it was a border town from which one could reach Los Angeles in a few hours by train or car, and although it had been declared the capital of the Northern District of Baja California in 1915, it was peaceful, far from the upheavals taking place in the rest of the Mexican Republic. Another attractive feature was it geographic proximity to Sonora, not to mention their similar climate and desert landscapes, which the Bernals missed a great deal. Another compelling factor was that business competition

The Bernal López family in the 1920s in Compuertas, Mexicali. Facundo, pictured here holding a mandolin, sits beside his brother Francisco, a fellow poet and journalist. Photo courtesy of Gabriel Trujillo Muñoz.

was scarce, and the border market demanded clothing for the city's growing population.

Pedro, who took on all the financial risk for this venture, decided that Facundo and Francisco would run the new business. Before leaving, Facundo married Rosaura Metzler, a young woman from Sonora who was living in Los Angeles. Her bloodline was profoundly *mestizaje*: Yaquis, Spanish, and German. Immediately after their marriage, Facundo and Rosaura, accompanied by Pedro and Francisco, took the train to the border. The entire family gathered on the platform to say farewell and wish them luck. Although they did not suspect this, their days of wandering were coming to an end.

Pedro and Facundo arrived at their destination on November 27, 1917. Mexicali would remain their place of residence for their rest of their lives. The business they started — the first of a long chain of clothing outlets, shoe stores, and suit emporiums — was called "Trajes a la Medida," and located next to Hotel del Norte, just south of the international border and in the very commercial heart of Mexicali. This was a bonanza period in the valley of Mexicali, but it was fleeting. The coming years would see the collapse of the cotton market, the principal regional crop; social tension between Chinese immigrants and Mexican residents; the lamentable practices of the Colorado River Land Company, the American corporation that essentially owned the valley; as well as political upheaval under the rule of General Esteban Cantú (1881-1966), whose regime in Baja was terminated in 1920.

But even with the economic setbacks and political troubles, the 1920s saw Mexicali grow and expand. Facundo and Rosaura contributed to these changes by having five daughters, all of them proud *Mexicalenses:* Obdulia, Ofelia, Angelina, Estela, and Margarita. Once the businesses were consolidated, Pedro and Ricardo kept them running, while Facundo returned to journalism and literature, especially after 1923, with the arrival of General Abelardo L. Rodríguez (1889-1967) as the Governor of the Northern District. Both Facundo and the General were of Sonoran origin, and they also shared the same pragmatic and mercantile spirit.

Mexicali was a young city when the Bernal brothers settled there. Its newspaper tradition was even younger: two years prior to their arrival, the city had seen the founding of its first newspaper, *El Noticiero del Distrito,* which was actually printed in the nearby city of Imperial, California. The first true native newspaper was *La Vanguardia*, which first appeared in 1917. General Cantú himself was its owner. Ever since, journalism in Baja California has been the tool of those in power. That being said, there was never a lack of opposing voices in the press, nor a dearth of newspapers critical of mainstream politics.

The real boom in publishing occurred under General Rodríguez. No fewer than 31 publications were founded under his rule, including *El Boletín Municipal* (which lasted from June to September 1925) and *El Fantasma*, a vaudeville paper (which lasted from December 1926 to August 1927). Both of these were published by Facundo and Francisco. Once again, as in Los Angeles, Francisco and Facundo were reunited in the shared task of journalism and literature. On December 20, 1923, Facundo published his satirical broadside *El Rey Momo*. Later, General

Rodríguez provided him with the capital necessary to create the Imprenta Nacional (National Printing Press). When Francisco arrived to manage the print shop, he arranged so that it would also serve as a bookstore. When business was slow, the brothers would compose editorials and poems.

Facundo also became a correspondent for *El Heraldo de México*, a Spanish-language newspaper that was published in Los Angeles and circulated in Mexicali, as well as a correspondent for metropolitan papers like *Excélsior* and *El Universal*. Consequently, much of his poetry — especially the work he published in *El Heraldo de México* — dealt with the preoccupations and problems of Mexican immigrants in the United States.[12] One must not forget that, during the 1920s, readers in the border region of Baja California were more concerned with what occurred in Los Angeles, San Diego, and the Imperial Valley, where large numbers of their friends and family resided, than with events in the country's interior.

It is this journalistic climate that gave rise to *A Stab in the Dark*. But let us have Facundo himself recount the editorial adventure that was the publication of his first and only collection of poetry.

Translated by Anthony Seidman

---

12   Since the mid-19th century, Spanish-language newspapers in California regularly featured verse on a variety of topics. See *The World of Early Chicano Poetry, 1846-1910*, vol. 1, *California Poetry,1855-1881*, edited by Luis A. Torres (Encino, CA: Floricanto Press, 1994) and *Hispanic Poetry in Los Angeles 1850-1900: La poesía angelina*, edited by Reynaldo Ruiz (Lewiston, N.Y.: Edwin Mellen Press, 2000).

A STAB IN THE DARK

No Godfather

WHAT HAPPENED to this book is something like what occurs with an infant born between life and death; lacking a godfather, it is baptized by the parents, that is to say, holy water is poured over the little thing so that it won't become another problem among the billions of immigrants in Limbo...

The baptism in this case is the prologue, and the godfather is a beloved friend and stylish writer who, because of last minute complications, perhaps found himself unable to comply with Christian duty.

And in such a frenzied trance, with 3,000 copies of the book ready to be bound and shipped deep into Mexican territory, I have set off on a drunken binge of pages, with the aim of advising the "patient" reader to ignore the bad appearance of this oeuvre, of which, as in Moratín's epigram, one can only say: "her best feature is her figure"[13]; and after going up and down the well-worn path covered by all prologues, I find myself in the same spot; tell me whether the following lines fail to observe the established formula. With or without a prologue, the sensible reader will perceive whatever is good or bad inside this book .

There you go... an apology de rigueur.

I have given this book the title *A Stab in the Dark* because its pages were written hastily, without an established order, as they were destined to fill the columns of a daily newspaper; a title that could be applied to many aspects of modern journalism, since the editors need to incubate their ideas in the heat of the day's current events, with the nervous tension produced by typesetters asking for "copy," or, just as often, to implore the rebellious Muses who have gone on strike to relent and give birth...

And so, here are my poor and blind stabs at the dark; let the reader receive them, knowing full well what they are: coarsely

---

13 Leandro Fernández de Moratín (1760-1828) was a prominent neo-classical Spanish dramatist and poet.

cut spears, chopped up at random, useless, except perhaps as serving for fuel, as purification from all sin. Amen.

August 1923
Los Angeles, Calif.

Míster BLIND
(Facundo Bernal)

PART I

La Prensa. **Evening Paper**

LA PRENSA has transformed
itself overnight
into a paper that distinguishes
wrong from right.
It has brought great surprise
to the Mexican people
and those who share the mother tongue.
It honors us all equally
while we flip through its pages,
    without shouting "Watch Out!"
La Prensa arrives; now it's a daily,
and if you don't believe me,
here, with your permission,
you can read our first edition!
And although the truth is never kind,
one must pardon the fright
upon gleefully diving into
truth that ultimately proves beautiful!
        That's right, gentlemen, we're a daily!
Whether you like it or not,
the change was called-for,
however much some adversary
might tell us, "This doesn't seem too..."
if he whines he's a coward,
lacking honor, lacking shame;
without shouting this from some rooftop,
it's the only evening edition!
Starting today, *La Prensa*:
groundbreaking because of its sources,
its effective opportunism,
its original articles,
and because each section
exudes *Mexicanismo.*
Because calumny rejects what's false,
and always triumphantly bears

the holy ideal that embraces:
THE HOMELAND AND ITS PEOPLE!
And as a motto: ONWARDS!
      Take this reprimand
flung our way by some cocky scoundrel
Who attempts, somehow, to diss
us, and let him wrap his mind around this:
he'd better not stir up a ruckus with us.
In that same section
and in meter & rhyme, no less,
I'm going to make a hobby
out of whacking him
daily and nightly with my sharpened cane...!
      And for now I ask
from my kind readers
the deepest forgetting
if some find themselves wounded
by these treacherous blows,
as I issue this plea
by my glistening pupils:
don't groan if I stab you all,
forgive a poor blind man
lacking a Lazarillo to heed his call.

June 18, 1922
Los Angeles, Calif.

Ah, that Don Félix!

The newspapers claim
that your perennially
presidential
Don Félix Díaz
has entered Mexico,
bent on igniting anew
the Revolution (?),
hoping, by that ho-hum strategy,
to achieve his dream
of becoming President.
Is poor Don Félix
completely blind to facts?
His delirious plots
have always failed him.
Hasn't the White House
told him their *No no no*'s,
because they don't want
Más Revoluciones?
And he keeps on beating his chest,
and instead of shriveling up,
the so-called Hero swells;
and when he faints
he makes me think of
the "Saint" from the Ciudadela...
And yet he struts forth,
bent on igniting anew
the Revolution (?);
he's one who counts on
Pablo González,
Pancho Murguía,
and other generals,
the types who now reside
in foreign lands,
gazing at the bulls,
but from behind the barrier,

because they imagine that
Don Félix will shortly return
from wherever he went,
to come and strum that tired tune
of bringing back
the Revolution (?)
down Mexico way...
Hoping, by that ho-hum strategy,
to achieve his dream
of becoming President.
Let Don Félix,
convince "the Gang"
of Zúñiga y Miranda
to enlist on his side.
Meanwhile, let him seek
a decent way
of earning a buck abroad.
And if misfortune
keeps him up at night,
let him invoke the memory
of the Ciudadela...
But don't let him
keep on attempting
to ignite anew
the Revolution (?)...

June 21, 1922
Los Angeles, Calif.

Félix Díaz (1868-1945) was a Mexican general and politician who participated in the rebellion against Madero during the Mexican Revolution. He escaped Ciudadela fortress, where he was serving a life sentence, during the "Ten Tragic Days" ("*La Decena Trágica*") between February 9 and February 19, 1913, which led up to the assassination of Madero and the installation of Victoriano Huerta as the 35th President of Mexico.

Huerta's reign was tumultuous and brief; he resigned and fled the county in 1914. Among Félix Díaz's most reliable supporters were General Pablo González (1879-1950), the chief organizer of the assassination of Emiliano Zapata (1879-1919), and General Francisco "Pancho" Murguía (1873-1922). Nicolás Zúñiga y Miranda (1865-1925) was an eccentric Mexican politician who ran for the presidency many times, without success, but insisted that he was in fact the "legitimate president."

Raking up the Past

They say the righteous judge
starts by keeping his
own house in order. Others claim
that one falls by one's own hands.
And just as those brief and useful
sayings are taken entirely from experience,
(let Sancho Panza repeat them...),
reader, I wish to apply them
to the same old problems,
and to dedicate a few "stabs"
to the people of my *Raza*
who leave Mexico, and when they've
barely set foot in Yankee-landia,
forget their Spanish
and disown their Homeland.
I am especially referring
to that plague that shamelessly
exploits their fellow countrymen,
and as those types
come in so many shapes and sizes,
so as not to bore the public,
I'll offer but one exhibit:
the cutesy-pie women from my land
who wear extra-short skirts,
and dance the "Hula-Hula,"
and smear on makeup,
and abscond with their beaus
and bathe in the sea,
and chew gum, and express themselves
in the language of Byron,
because they no *hablan* "Spanish."
I'll say it again to the women from my land,
take care to cover your sex —
I don't wish to tell them more.
And because I know that they're

fully Mexican — knowing them well —
I don't wish to allude to
the very hoity-toity older women
who remark about Mexico
(O Lord!), "I won't even look in that direction,
until things change";
they go on about the female "diplomats"...
but I don't wish to discuss them...
out of respect for their gray hairs,
and let their Exquisite Sexes rest in peace.
Instead, I lift my lance against those renegades
who include themselves in the *Raza*
of Juárez and Bolívar
only when it benefits them.
Take this example: the end-point of
the bull-run that winds up
seeming like a scam;
the famous healers
who cure whatever they desire
through various means...
just to score some dough;
certain professional lodges
(not those from Hispano-America,
nor others that prove virtuous),
that exploit our *Raza*
in exchange for certain offers,
hare-brained dreams, and hopes,
Jewish grifters and
wholesale jewelry merchants;
Certain employment agencies
who hook the guileless nitwit
with the promise of ten bucks per day,
firewood, electricity, room and board,
and they say that the job's
just ten miles away
and then reveal that they're really
sending them to Calipatria

to pick watermelon beneath the blaze
of the sun, for a pittance.
Against all of those people,
(if I can even consider them human)
and many others I don't mention here,
I raise my lance,
defending what's rightly ours —
FOR THE HOMELAND AND THE PEOPLE.
And here I place a full stop...
Until the next show...

Compatriots at the Beach

1. Getting Ready

"Come on, Timotea,
help me brush and part my hair
so that, in a little while,
we can go to the beach.
Hand me my
olive-colored shirt
and my purple
socks. Quick, iron
my pants.
Oh! And my silk handkerchief..."
"You're a real pain in the neck!"

2. On the Streetcar

"Hop on, Timotea,
the streetcar's moving,
hold on tight.
Hurry, Chemalía,
the train's leaving without us!
Jesus, it's a tight squeeze.
We barely fit.
Ouch! Watch out, stupid!
He popped one of my blisters!
What a mammoth!
May lightning strike him dead!"

3. At the Seaside Resort

"Holy Mother
and Virgin! Just look at them,
parading in their birthday suits!
Who would believe it?
No wonder they call
this place the 'Be-atch'..."
"Let's see if you shut up!
Here, Timotea,
everything's natural,
everything's pleasing...
Nothing seems wrong."
"I can't believe my eyes!
Look at Doña Chona
in a bathing suit
with her baby bump...
Come on, Chemalía,
let's get out of here,
or the same 'accident'
will happen to me."
"Lord, Timotea
you're so prudish,
any little old thing
shocks you."
"Well, I just don't get
this fashion. What do you want from me?
Maybe if it was for men,
and not women...
Don't you agree with me,
Chemalía?"
"No, because fashion...
well... it's soon out of fashion..."

4. At the Carnival Games

"Damn it! Nothing
but bad luck.
I lost a lousy
ten dollar bill
playing Cupid."
"Hey, you'll never win.
Whatever the house grabs,
it keeps."

5. At the Dance Hall

"Jesus! That music
they play at the dance hall —
Blind Simon's orchestra
had them all beat.
See how they stretch
and tuck in their legs
in the blink of an eye?
Like little tin monkeys!"
"Old Lady, if anything,
they show great restraint —
way back when, you'll recall,
they would dance cheek to cheek."

6. On the Rollercoaster

"Our Lady of Aid!"
"I'm holding you tight —
Honey, this ride
is sure to kill us!
Lord, how it shoots up!
Lord, how it shoots down!"
"I feel my guts squashing
up against my jaws."
"Hey, *Míster*, stop it...
Se...se...se...señor...
For Goodness' sake...
Do me the favor.
Hold on to me, Chémali,
it's shooting down again..."
"Argh! Feels like the wind
got knocked out of me."
"Finally! The goddamn
car's stopped."
"You don't wanna go
again, Timotea?"
"Me?
I'd rather die
than come back here!
"Fine —
suit yourself..."

A Sermon

My much beloved daughters
and sisters in Jesus Christ:
our Mother Church instructs us,
who act as Ministers,
to guide the faithful
along the righteous path.
And to remove from their way
those obstacles and dangers
that sow temptation
in weak spirits.
Let us watch over our neighbor
as we do over ourselves,
and in the end, let us remain
faithful representatives of Christ.
Because of this, my daughters,
(later, I'll address my sons),
I will give you some guidance,
which will save you from the Stalker
and Enemy of Virtue,
the Protector of Vice.
Much beloved daughters:
with nothing but love I instruct you
to lengthen the hems of your skirts,
even if only by an inch or two;
for I see on these streets
of God, beautiful hearts of palm
ranging in age from 16 to 20,
and in some cases even 40-something
(please excuse my irreverence)...
judging them based on their
exposed bodies, one would think
they still ask for candy
and to ride piggyback.

Do not paint your faces
with those vivid cosmetics
that render your charm ugly;
do not abuse your physique;
do not frequent those dances
with such... ah... ridiculous cleavages,
which expose what should
remain forever unseen;
do not dance to certain pieces
whose suggestive swaying
ignites temptation
among novice dancers;
if you dance, do so
with enough space between each other,
(dancing, in my judgment,
is a fitting form of entertainment
and a healthy exercise
that invigorates one's limbs,
relaxes the spirit,
as long as one doesn't cross the line
of good taste);
because I know of certain couples
who, despite what's been deemed
forbidden by recent decrees,
will even dance the "Hula-Hula"
without giving a hoot
about why it was censored
by far wiser, wizened minds.
I will leave for a future sermon,
my beloved daughters,
my thoughts on the habit
of swimming in public places,
where modesty is shipwrecked
while sin sails forth.
In the name of the Father,
and the Holy Ghost,
Amen. Here I make the sign of the cross

with total veneration,
and "until I regard You, O Christ."
Receive the blessings
of your father:

FRIAR-TORIBIO

Better off Being Chinese

Dear Reader, after a prolonged hiatus
of three days,
I return to my bitter task
of talking trash
against those of our ilk
who disown their ancestors
in a most inhuman manner,
then set themselves up
as model Bad Mexicans.

Today, I'll take a stab
at the "Reactionaries,"
the ones who regard "Don Félix" as a God.
To give you a taste of them, here
are two of the most outlandish exemplars.

"Things will surely
change. It's certain
that Don Félix is in Mexico,
and one must roll up one's sleeves...
Because these are urgent times...
He can count on a thousand
prestigious (?) Generals,
who come from the ranks
of the old *Federales*, with 500 officials,
and 120 soldiers.

And with a similar troop,
the *Caudillo*
can conquer Europe,
as easily as he might down
a cup of cod liver oil."

"The bad thing is
he didn't get the Okay

from Washington. What a mess!"
"True that! The more he offered them,
The more they ignored him."

"However, if there is no Victory
for now,
we will prevail later;
five years, or even a decade,
are nothing when it comes to History…
We will march forward
and against the Revolution;
Let it come…
the Intervention.
We need to hit rock bottom
for the Reaction to prevail.

And if that day never comes,
I would prefer
to lose my citizenship."
"I too would rather
end my days as a foreigner."

(The two of them, in chorus):
"With Don Félix, we are Mexicans,
but without him, we'd rather be
Chinese, North Americans,
English… even the very
compatriots of Lucifer."

"Things will surely
change. It's certain
that Don Félix is in Mexico,
and one must roll up one's sleeves…
Because these are urgent times…"

José Fonseca

Kind Reader,
I call time-out
to all this "parrying,"
and offer some fitting
words of praise
to the most fearless,
to the most daring
of our heroes
from the Air Force:
I'm alluding
to the celebrated
Mexican Aviator,
(just saying his name
feels so good),
José Fonseca.
He soared up in "Venís"!
Those daring,
electrifying flights!
Hey, you! Look at him!
He rises, serene
and steady,
smiles at the public,
then rocks back &
forth across the airstreams;
he toys with death
and sows panic
among the spectators.
Look: all of a sudden
he inscribes a "loop de loop,"
and then just hangs there,
by his claws,
though he has nothing
to clutch;
and that's how he

tries his luck,
steady and indifferent
to Death.

Twenty thousand souls
Have trekked to Venís
to witness the exploits
of our hero, who,
this coming Sunday,
will offer new stunts,
which he reserves
for the most solemn occasions.

Glory to our Countryman!
Honor to the Hero!
For he justly deserves
honor and glory.
Such countrymen as he
honor Mexico
in the highest degree...
where we
are so poorly understood...
and show that they know
how to smile
in the face of Death!...

According to a report in the *Los Angeles Times*, on Sunday, June 11, 1922, José Fonseca, "formerly captain of aviation in the Mexican army," performed a series of aerial stunts at the Ince Flying Field in Venice, California. He went up in a De Havilland DH.4 two-seat biplane with a pilot named Frank Clark, and while Clark "executed a loop-the-loop," Fonseca "hung by his toes from the bar connecting two wheels of the landing gear." But what made this "the more remarkable," the *Times* journalist wrote, was Fonseca's "physical condition":

He was nine times wounded in the revolutionary fighting and most of the bullets were lead slugs that tore the bone. His left arm was carried away at the shoulder and although it was patched up he has almost no use of it. His left leg also is permanently injured, but he can use it fairly well. One bullet pierced his lung, two shattered the right shoulder and another broke the skull.

"Is... Real... Stunt... Flyer," *Los Angeles Times*, 12 June 1922: 9.

The Radio

"Words from over there, coming here,
words from here, going there;
if they find one another on the roadway
how many times will they crash...?"

Everyone's become a boob
due to the new device
that transmits the Hertz waves:
the Radio... It marvelously
receives them from
distant points.
Thus, music, song,
and other noises
are heard clearly
and distinctly, so that
when they reach our ears,
it seems like we're drifting
in some fantastic dream.

Just yesterday, at last,
I could listen to this miracle
in the laboratory
of a kind countryman
and friend, who invited me over
and showed me the Radio,
and I tell you all,
hand over heart,
I was stunned —
I repeat, that new device
is astonishing;
yet everything that's good
has a bad side to it as well,
and being such a Wonder,

you can expect the radio to have its faults,
and to prove this to you all,
I offer two cases.

Mrs. X
attempts to listen
to a broadcast of the *Examiner*,
but, oh!, upon trying to do so,
she clearly makes out the voice
of her husband, Don Mariano,
conversing next to a transmission
device.
"Come on,"
says that shameless man,
"let's go to Venice —
it's already a quarter past six;
we'll dine together,
and then come back —
after enjoying ourselves."
And then a woman's voice
responds, in that same scene,
"But you're married...
And if your wife finds out
about this... Christ!
What would she say?" "My wife?
She can go to hell!"

Days later, the expensive
half of Don Mariano
files for divorce. All
because of the cursed Radio...

"Woman, it's already eight o'clock,
and I haven't had a bite to eat.
I got here at five
wiped out from work,
and instead of cooking me

some supper — dammit! —
you're listening to gossip,
to music and jingles!"
"Quiet! Don't make noise,
Lázaro is singing..."
"Get into that kitchen
on the double,
or you'll be left with no husband —
and just that device to snuggle with!..."

Of course, dear Reader,
it goes without saying,
such things would never happen
to *our* cousins... *our* brothers.

"Lázaro" in the penultimate stanza refers to Hipòlit (or Hipólito) Lázaro (1887-1974), a Spanish-born operatic tenor who was very popular in Latin America.

Prophets of Doom

When Mr. De la Huerta
left for New York
to make arrangements
with the bankers
regarding foreign debt,
the enemies of Mexico,
the Reactionary Tigers,
laughed scornfully
and raised their voices,
predicting complete failure
for our Minister,
because he wasn't a mover-and-shaker,
(and lacked the "ad hoc" guts),
unlike that genius of finance
who was known by the name of "Limantour,"
a genius that Don Luis Cabrera
knew he could count on...
and they shouted blindly:
"De la Huerta's on his way to New York?
He's dealing with the big-shot
financiers? Ha! What a nightmare!
The surprises we're gonna get
from the Obregón administration!"
And so they continued
talking trash,
those enemies of Mexico,
the Wolves of the Reaction.

Now that Mr. De la Huerta,
lacking the "ad hoc" guts,
and ignorant of the financial sciences,
which not even "Limantour"
could employ and put our debt afloat,
has brought prestige and honor
to our Homeland, those very

Jackals of the Reaction,
blinded by spite,
try to blot out the sun
with their fingers, insisting
Mexico failed,
and that if there had been an arrangement,
it was made under conditions
bound to prove a "grave sacrifice"
to the Nation...
They keep on barking at the moon,
those Canines of the Reaction,
dreaming of a miracle,
of a better existence...

Adolfo de la Huerta (1881-1955) served as the 38th President of Mexico from June 1 to November 30, 1920, and was succeeded by Álvaro Obregón (1880-1928), who won the 1920 election. He became the Secretary of Finance and Public Credit and negotiated the De la Huerta-Lamont Treaty of 1922, which consolidated Mexico's many debts and paved the way for normalized relations with the United States and other nations. Luis Cabrera (1876-1954) served as the Secretary of Finance and Public Credit under Venustiano Carranza, the 37th President of Mexico, while José Yves Limantour (1854-1935) was the Secretary of Finance under the Porfirio Díaz regime, from 1893 to 1911.

The Crime Wave

In this divine city
of beachside resorts
and parks brimming
with lush lakesides,
in the beautiful Angelo-polis,
which is covered
by the cloak of fog
as white as a bull's eye,
I discovered
a handcuffed woman,
for the crimson wave of crime
has flooded over us
and is sowing
Terror and Horror
among the Decent Folk.
Today, two or three Apaches
rob a bank
in broad daylight, and then
two youths assault
the post office
or a "Wells & Fargo";
and now the victim's a lady
shot dead by some punks
for no clear motive,
but according
to their statement,
they were instructed by Spirit X
or perhaps the Devil himself.
The "Bluebeards"
bob along a blood-river,
and just now a remorseless dame
has confessed
that she's been married ten times,
and that every one of her unsuspecting
ex-husbands

was baked to a crisp
in the oven
she reserves for such delicacies.

But none of these occurrences
sparked as much outrage
as the headlines
from three days past:
La Prensa got the scoop
about this horrendous crime:
the tragic gust
of jealousy snuffs out
"the will-o'-the-wisp
of Reason." An arm
is raised in threat —
gaze upon it! In its white
and ivory-smooth hand
it carries Death. Beneath it,
a women begs for mercy
in vain.
Suddenly, and as violently
as a lightning bolt,
the arm falls upon
the unfortunate one
and deals a horrendous
blow to her cranium:
a bloody flower blossoms
beneath the crime's
spasm. And then another blow,
and another, another,
until all that's left
are dirty chunks
slicked with blood,
and splattered
with brain matter.
Gruesome tableau!
A lady asks to borrow

another woman's car
to take a spin,
but is premeditating
her murder, because she thinks
this woman
has seduced her husband.

And she carries out
her plan... She kills her
with a hammer!

For more on the crime described in the last two stanzas, see note
to "In Defense of Phillips."

Bruno's Mother-In-Law

My friend Bruno Valente
writes to me from Santa Paula,
bitterly complaining
about his mother-in-law;
in short, he feels like
a bird trapped in a cage,
or so he says,
ever since his black luck,
or perhaps the Devil himself,
who disintegrates everything,
mixed his mother-in-law
into his happy marriage.

But let's give Bruno
his say,
and you will all see
how that rascal
complains like no one else
about conjugal life.

"Tomorrow, it will be exactly
a year since I married Teodora,
a delightful girl
who had the poor taste
to call herself my wife.

And geez, how we love one another,
so much so, there's nothing more to say;
when we think of throwing in the towel,
we can't, and then we don't even eat
because we soar in passionate flight.

'You're my only rapture!'
'My Kuppie!'
'My lil' chickpea!'

'Give me another kiss… and another…'
'Another kiss!'
We devote the entire day
to such sweet 'intermezzo.'

But as soon as we reach
absolute joy,
our hopes suddenly sink —
we glimpse signs
of a fast-approaching storm.

For it was either my black luck
or perhaps the Devil himself,
who disintegrates everything,
that sought to mix my mother-in-law
into my happy marriage.

She comes and goes, and goes
and comes, according to her will,
screaming at anyone in her way.
What a woman! Holy Virgin!
She's a bitch on wheels.

Oh! In her rage, my mother-in-law
bats the shrews' World Record
and wins first place. I'm more scared
of her than I am of a bull from Piedras Negras.

Ever since that virago
set foot in my home,
she named herself Judge and Chief,
making of me a pathetic putz,
a perfect good-for-nothing.

Her blood boils if I say too little;
if I talk too much, she raises her voice;
if I sing, she says I'm a nutcase;

if I smoke, I make her woozy;
in short, she's got me by the balls!

If I go out, she chews me out;
if I stay in, she won't give me the time of day;
if things continue like this,
I'm going to give her a taste of my rifle.

Yes, I'm on the verge of killing her;
can happen anytime... hang her... a bit of cyanide...
or maybe a trusty hammer...
whatever's the cheapest way
to get out of this jam.

Later they'll learn of a son-in-law
who had suffered from blackest grief,
but has freed himself from Hell
by murdering his mother-in-law
in the modern manner."

And at the end of his missive,
poor Bruno sketches out
the following moral,
in which he advises us
in a most expressive manner:

"If you procure a life mate,
because she's right up your alley,
or because the Devil wished it so,
hold on to her, whomever she may be...
as long as she has no mother...!"

The Spiritualists from Bacerac

The press
reported how
in Sonora
there live two
intriguing,
pretty, and sweet
young women,
harassed by
the spirits;
day and night
these spirits
torment the ladies
with strange
suggestions;
they pinch
the ladies,
they stop
the ladies when
they're out strolling.
When the ladies
sit down at table —
blessed Virgin! —
they feel some-
one's breath
on the napes of their
necks when they
least expect it.
All of the dishes
in the kitchen
fly from the shelves
and shatter
into tiny shards.
When they're
in bed,

they hear
terrifying
imprecations,
curses
that give them
goosebumps,
followed by singing
and laughter,
and then —
tickling!
Naturally,
those poor victims
of the spirits
of Bolshevism
are left clueless;
and they too
will end up
as spirits
if their troubles
don't cease.
But lucky them!
A respectable
capitalist
who dabbles
in Spiritualism
is willing
to send them
to the metropolis,
so that doctors
may study
this rare case.

The oddest
bit of the news
is that serious
people lend credence
to the claim,

saying they too
have witnessed
these events —
or so say
the reporters,
who would never,
ever fib...

Although folks
may laugh this off
as a joke,
the case *is* serious:
two intriguing,
pretty, and sweet
young women
are being harassed
and don't know
who's doing it...
They need help,
on the double!
Call a doctor
or a Spiritualist!

It's Because We Be from "Back There"

"Ya' Honor,
I asked to see you
to beg Your
Excellenty
if he could give me
that job that just opened up
cuz' Manuel Escalante
got a promotion.
You can have a look
at the letter
of recommendation
and the references I've got;
they talk about my
Aptitudes and Behavior."
The Boss looks
over the papers,
then says:
"You're a young man
who hasn't achieved
his potential. Tell me,
what's your status?"
"Sir, I'm single."
"Your place of birth?"
"I'm from Jalisco."
"Well... that's gonna be a problem."
"Why's that?"
"Might as well drop it;
I'm terribly sorry,
but there's no opening."

Sir, here's a reference
that needs your signature.
"Hold on a moment.
There. Come in. So,
what skills have you got?"

"I've 'writing' and 'reading'
pretty well down —
oh, and 'counting' —
so *correctfully*, might I add,
that I can tell
when the rooster's about to crow."
"Know shorthand?
Can ya compose a letter?
Can ya typewrite?"
"I know enough
To get started."
"Now tell me:
Is your status, er, 'local'?"
"Yep! Sonora is my state-tus!"
"Hell, you shoulda started
with that!"
Consider yourself
hired!"

Dry or Wet?

"It's dry everywhere
in Yankee-landia;
the Volstead Act
sent wine and winos
straight to hell:
a truly sagacious law,
and an exemplary one.
Thanks to it,
we don't suffer from
a tavern
at every 20 feet,
nor the freak show
of drunken
men and women
zigzagging about.
And on Sundays
the drunks don't travel
by the hundreds
on the streetcars,
to reach Vernon,
way out there,
where, back in the day,
such caravans
would find
their watering holes...
Neither do we see
such "beach scenes"
as back in the day,
when myriad wasted
men and women
engaged in sexcapades,
buck naked,
under the boardwalk.
Nowadays, everyone
feels good.

far from the reach
of that horrendous vice...
That's what I said
to Mister Benson,
my neighbor,
a real party animal,
who's always
(what's that expression?)
"three sheets to the wind."
He responded
by making an obscene gesture,
then stated:
"Listen, neighbor,
what're ya talkin' about?
You think there ain't no wine?
Ain't no drunkards out there?
Ya tryin' to pull my leg?
Listen: now that we're 'dry,'
there're more alkies
than ever before.
It's only
that we're drinkin' less,
because the "sauce"
is much stronger
and it drains
the wallet dry.
Don't you see the boozers,
men and women,
out on the streets,
just like before? Sure:
now there are lil' shops
of drinks that pack a punch,
good stuff, inside
every rundown hotel;
1,500 of them,
where guys and gals
can get blatto,

which is now called
'lookin' out for yourself.'
On the other hand,"
he continued
in a bitter tone,
"without the usual
tax on the sweet stuff,
it's the government
that's on the losing end.
Deprived of millions,
and with no way
of getting back
what it used to rake in,
they're raising taxes
up to seventh heaven —
leaving us citizens
to foot the bill."

Here we leave
Mister Benson
behind a semicolon;
Well, we foreigners
living in Yankee-landia,
have nothing but respect
for your Rules and Regulations,
be they good or bad.

Pochos

In the U.S. there's a lot
of good to imitate,
in terms of Truth and Justice
and the Honor System.
To cite just one thing
for example,
there's the Work Ethic,
and the desire to save
every nickel and dime
with amazing skill,
as capital kindly permits —
a habit that becomes
a safeguard against the future,
which is always uncertain,
whether your collar's
blue or white.

I could cite some
other examples here,
but what I've already provided
should suffice, and make it evident
that I speak impartially.

I now wish to focus on
those from back home
who land here, observe things,
and never imitate what's good,
but only what's terrible.
No need to beat around the bush
when it comes to describing them.
What's fair is fair.

But before starting with them,
allow me to sketch a new
and original case.

Say, you see that young man
chewing…what could he be chewing?
Must be tobacco or gum;
makes no difference, for our purposes.
He is accompanied by his "little lady" —
not much meat on her bones, underage
(even a blind man can see that) —
 whose angelic face
(and I use that adjective in quotes)
has been buried beneath
makeup and rouge; her skirt
allows me to glimpse
the exact position of her garters,
which move farther and farther,
like "seabirds (sorry to wax
poetic!) in steady flight"
Her cleavage nearly
reveals all, *au naturel*,
and… Shoot! I almost forgot
that I'd promised to shut my trap
about the "weaker sex";
once again, I kindly beseech them
to overlook the slips
of my fading memory.

Taking advantage of their pardon,
let me continue,
as I haven't yet satisfied
all my curiosity about the tender
couple I'd mentioned
some lines back.
I want to eavesdrop… I approach
them…and I listen:

 "'*All right*,'
call me on the 'telephone'…

My number's '*Ayt one seven Oh three nine*'...
Then you can tell me if you '*got*'
that '*guy Sam*' to loan you '*ees aromobil*,'
so we can go our
for a '*ride*' in style
down by the '*bitch-ees*'..."
"You know wha', Marry?
And don't get upset, '*sweetheart*,'
by what I'm gonna tell ya' —
'I dunno' if we can go."
"What?
So, you're that '*cheep*,' are ya?
Figures... '*sun-ah-va-gún*'...
Why'd I bother gettin' ready, made-up?
'*What su mara?*' '*Cheeses Cries!*'

At that very moment (cruel fate!),
an ambulance races by,
sirens blaring, and I
can't hear another word.

And since I'm out of material,
I guess it's time for a period.

Short Films

I'll provide a quick rendering
of our surroundings,
which will give shape and color
to the "main drag,"
located between
"First" and the Plaza —
of "New High" and "Alameda,"
and other avenues of dubious stature,
where our fellow countrymen
who don't know a thing about
these new surroundings
get easily fleeced
by merciless swindlers.

"For the price of ten pesos
you'll be dressed to the nines!
Try on this coat, Sir.
Look: what fine lining!
Great: a bit higher...

Looks dandy from the front!"
(The tailor pulls it down
six inches at the back.)
"Now look in the mirror:
Such an *elegant* cut!"
(Now the old dog pulls back
six inches from the sides.)
And if there's no one there to warn
our countryman, he's screwed;
he's just bought a suit
for Fatty from the flickers.

"This watch, here, is pure silver,
and it comes with a hundred-year warranty."
(And a one-day lifespan!)

"Come on in and listen to the pianola.

Won't cost ya a thing!"
(They enter and it's over —
they get taken to the cleaners!)

"Four greenbacks for each bet."
"The game's done."
"I've lost so much,
I feel hung over."

The last line of the third stanza, "Fatty from the flickers" ("*El Gordito del cine*" in the original Spanish), is likely a reference to Fatty Arbuckle (1887-1933), whose trials for the rape and man-slaughter of Virginia Rappe (1895-1921) scandalized the public in 1921 and 1922.

Short Films, Redux

"There's dough to be made in pickin' cotton!
Five bucks, cash money, for every 220 pounds!"
(So they set off to the Imperial Valley
and try their luck...)

"Your eyes seduce me,
you enchanting lil' thing."
(They drink lemonade
and converse for half an hour.)

"You hear that Christian hymn, my fellow grifter?"
"Come on in! We take the best family
portraits! Cheap! Very cheap!"
(And they leave without a penny.)

Here's another
catalog of clients,
because the linotypists
are asking for new ones.

What's It to Me?

So. Both national
and foreign
railroaders have gone on strike,
and the government wants
to hang 'em for any old reason?
What's it to me?

So. The prosecutor's witnesses
give Lady Justice
much heartache
with stories of the bloody crime,
because they saw the incident.
What's it to me?

So. Because all is permitted
and no one is fined,
bare-limbed bathers
parade on the shore.
Is that why "tourists"
like to go to the beach, to gawk?
What's it to me?

So. Fearing an awkward encounter,
a certain Mexican group
that wanted to invite us to coffee
has deserted the "Hispanic and
American Center."
What's it to me?

So. Some of my countrymen,
who look like troglodytes
and eat nothing but beans,
insist they're Iberian
and answer me with: "Wha' chu sey?"
What's it to me?

So. You're walking down "New High,"
and they tell you, "Good bye,"
then kick you in the ass,
knee you in the crotch,
and put you in a casket.
What's it to me?

So. Certain dames I know
wear short dresses,
abuse the color vermillion,
caking on powder, smearing lipstick,
and end up looking like "Kuppies."
What's it to me?

So. You purchase some pants
in a Department Store,
and when you try them on,
they seem like someone else's,
and you shout and curse.
What's it to me?

So. Two or three hustlers
evoke the "better days,"
out of "patriotism," and do "something"
to celebrate Don Hidaldgo,
so that people fork over some cash.
What's it to me?

So, this "ritornello"
makes some of my targets'
hair stand on end...
And if they decided
to get up in my face?
Well, that's a different matter.

Why There Are No Bells...

Everyone knows
that story
about the priest
who once went
to a certain town
and who didn't hear
any clanging:
he searched here
and there for a reason,
till a parishioner
told him,
with great faith:
"Well, Father,
I'll give you
three reasons
WHY THERE ARE NO BELLS —
first..."
Well,
that's enough
to know
the cause
of the absence.

A merchant
from this Babel
told me one day:
"I don't know what to do:
sales are down,
while taxes
keep going up,
and the rent, too,
keeps rising.
Just staying afloat

is a struggle.
How can I
solve this problem —
please tell me, sir?
And parodying
the parishioner
of the bells, I said:
'Well, your sales are nil
for three reasons.
One — because
you don't advertise. Two,
and also, three —
because you don't
advertise.
There you have them:
the three reasons
I gave him.

And if advertising
is the key to great sales,
word of mouth is great,
but the "papers"
(as they call them)
are a safer bet
for earning back
a hundred times
of what you spend
on a few square inches.

And if you run
an ad in *La Prensa*,
(cheap and classy
ads printed here),
you'll get rich

before you can count
one, two, three. *

July 27, 1922
Los Angeles, Calif.

Míster BLIND
(General Advertising Agent)

* *That is, if you run an advertisement at least two inches across*
three columns... more or less, it's your choice.

Landlords

The locals from this neighborhood
beg for mercy
from the unprecedented abuse
of the Lordly Landlords, who,
fearless of Hell's Vengeful Flames,
raise and raise the rents
until the monthly damage
reaches Seventh Heaven.
And the houses!
Dank shacks with barely
three rooms... 50 pesos a month!
And the rooms! Eternal Father!
A cramped living room,
its floor glued to its ceiling,
and a bedroom *en plein air*
(very hygienic, to be sure);
the kitchen is a cage
with the wind coming and going,
making itself at home, just like Pedro;
the "powder room" is just six feet
from where one eats. Add to those splendors
the constant clackety-clack
from the upstairs neighbors;
yes, the house I'm sketching
has two floors. The "toilet"
is a modern apparatus;
when it's working, it soaks
us, bathing our entire bodies;
moreover, there's the advantage
of waking up at the crack of dawn
without an alarm clock,
because the buzz of the bedbugs
will keep you red-eyed.

And don't you even think
about bringing your lil' tykes,
(although feel free to raise
parrots, cats, and dogs,
who all enjoy unalienable rights here);
but to even think
of bringing your children home...
Get thee gone!
Don't you do it! Otherwise
the Landlord will show up,
furious, saying the children
disturb the tenants' sleep,
saying the brats are scuffing
the floors, the walls, the ceiling...
And that's that, you'll need to
vacate premises before the first,
or your furniture will be tossed
to the curb, and now you're in a real bind,
just because you have kids
who haven't grown quickly enough...!

Would to Heaven there were
unions up here
that get practical results,
like those in Mexico...

Letter Sent from Mexico to Los Angeles, Calif.

"*Compadre* Tobías;
I respectfully send you this card
to notify you
That we're now living in Jauja,
ever since they promised us
land, peace, and water.
For honesty's sake, I tell you:
we don't earn dollars,
nor do the houses here
have porches, lil' lawns,
or other trifles;
none of those buildings
so tall you think they're
about to crumble
menace us as we walk about.
We have none of that
here, in our country;
But here, solid silver
handsome Aztecs
are in circulation;
as far as houses go
In our local "colonias,"
we've got plenty charming
"chalets" that, inside,
prove just as elegant.
And what about our palaces?
Whenever some foreigners
peer upon them,
they start drooling...
Either for good or ill,
we don't have
lush parklands
or radiant shores,
where the whitest flesh
is put on display...

However, we do
take delight in the divine
and splendid panoramas
of our mountains;
and there's Xochimilco,
(doesn't seem like much!),
and the "Woods," remnants
from our glorious past,
which we wouldn't trade for anything
(I swear on my mother's grave),
not even if dealing with Mister Wilson;
and we have so,
so many other things
in this blessed land
known as Anáhuac.
Come on down, *compadre*.
Although the pool
may be shrinking, grab
all the cash under your mattress,
and if that's not enough,
send us a letter stating
what you need... we'll help.
Answer ASAP.
Also, tell me what happened
to the 100 bucks
I sent for my house
when I was thinking of buying one.
La Prensa tipped us off
that the bank
where I deposited my dough
went belly up,
and left us,
the *Raza*,
gaping like gators...
Hope to hear from you soon.

Fondly... Accept
an embrace from your *compadre*,
Pedro Rodríguez Aranda."

Letter Sent from Los Angeles to Mexico

Dear *Compadre,*
your letter was delayed;
I opened it and it speaks of things
that reach straight to the heart:
with regards to Xochimilco,
that's where I have my four *chinampas*
and where an old woman awaits my return:
my dearest mother!
You speak to me of the woods,
the lakes and the mountains,
and the divine sky of Mexico —
see my tears
as I hear of these things:
they burst from deep within the soul.
Thank you for the tickets.
It's a pity that they can't give us
tickets like they used to...
just because some countrymen
insinuate things about others
and when the boats dock,
they beat us to the port;
they go to Mexico
but return after two weeks,
since they go just for fun,
while we, with our bags
packed and ready, remain here,
lurching in place...
How sweet it would be
for the Government to decree
repatriation for us, placing
the duty in honest hands...

With regards to the money matter,
there's nothing to be done;
the bank went bust... that's that...

It's closed for good.
Lawyers, a lot of them, are scheming,
seeing if a part of that shipwreck,
perhaps the hull, can be salvaged.
Don't keep your hopes up!
But keep on writing, you hear?
Don't get flustered, *compadre*.
Your letters of love and joy
belong in this home;
they bring with them the odor
of my lush *chinampas*,
along with memories of mother, and the Glory
enveloping my *Raza*.

Keep writing to me
about those things that reach
straight to the heart,
and receive a warm embrace
from your *compadre*:

Matías Lizárraga

PART II

The Suffocating Heat of Mexicali

The suffocating heat
from the igneous Imperial Valley
blasts infernal degrees
that make even the "Toughest"
mortal change colors.

The African sun, cradle
to the blackness of the "One-Day Flower" —
that sun is not a sun, but like a moon,
when compared to one single
sunblaze at noon
in this blesséd Valley
of Lamentations... and Sweat.

What else? Walk along the street
and after a couple steps, you're
certain to find two or three "Toughs,"
both of their hands empty,
bodies stiff as any old corpse;
if the Devil, on one of his many forays,
were to sojourn here for a day or two,
we would hear his death rattle.
And that's no exaggeration —
I'm telling you the plain truth:
in this scalding region,
the one who doesn't sweat,
is peeled by evaporation.

If you seek comfort
in the tub, you can bet
you'll get nothing
but a Russian Banya
and hair loss, unless you bathe
with bucketsful of ice.

Fleeing these heat waves,
which excite the body's system,
poor, bedeviled sweethearts
meet up in refrigerators
to discuss their trysts,
because once, a certain couple,
after sharing an ardent kiss
found that their lips
remained fused
between the window bars.

This hellish heat
makes us lose our minds;
just take a sniff (I mean it):
everyone here smells like
steak and blazing charcoal!...
If you place some fresh eggs
in a refrigerator, you're certain
to see them hatch in a half-hour...!

And what's worse, dear Reader,
in the hours of heat —
which are those of daylight
and moonlight — one observes
rare psychological phenomena.

An example: the Pedants
and the prideful Bankers
who would never greet one another,
turn into polite, if not
obsequious, acquaintances,
due to the searing temperatures;
this is understandable... during
the third stage of sunstroke,
when their spirits disintegrate,
they burn in sweet equality.

Another example: the political
providers of the Congress, on Sunday,
when dealing with severe cases:
these "fatties," "lankies," and "punies"
almost kiss one another on the lips...

So decide for yourself, dear Reader,
if the suffocating heat
of the igneous Imperial Valley
can't "change the color"
of the Toughest of mortals.

El Tecolote Ablaze

One mist-webbed night
a "tecolote" burned
and its body was consumed
without a feather singed...

After the blaze
a few days ago,
which also consumed
several houses
(let Monjo tell us,
and Doctor Molina,
those at the Monte Carlo,
and those next door,
and if they don't wish
to speak... so be it),
a new disaster
reduced one square block
to ashes: the area
where men gamble,
where "ladies of the night"
wait in their nooks.
The hotel of Arturo
Him Sam Lung fell victim
to the blaze;
but it was quickly doused.
Like a swarm of wasps,
1,500 Chinese armed with
pickaxes, pails, and frying pans,
succeeded in snuffing
the fire that would have
finished off all the children of China...
The great blaze started
(the case has an explanation),
near the suffocating red light
district. All of the water pumps

were in working order,
but neither the small nor
the large pumps could
put out the burning buildings.
Both homes and businesses
were reduced to rubble,
and now not even ashes
remain of the "bird of prey."
They're still estimating the losses.

El Tecolote, meaning "the owl" (the Mexican Spanish term is of Nahuatl origin), was a booming casino, brothel, and theater in Mexicali, which existed, with interruptions, from 1909 to 1925. Two of those interruptions were due to fires that destroyed the establishment in 1920 and in 1922. A headline in the *Los Angeles Times* on September 27, 1919, reporting on *El Tecolote*'s temporary closure, dubbed it the "Mexican Monte Carlo." See Eric Michael Schantz, "All Night at the Owl: The Social and Political Relations of Mexicali's Red-Light District, 1909-1925," in *On the Border: Society and Culture Between the United States and Mexico,* ed. Andrew Grant Wood (Lanham, MD: SR Books, 2004), pp. 91-144, and *idem,* "Meretricious Mexicali: Exalted Masculinities and the Crafting of Male Desire in a Border Red-Light District, 1908-1925," in *Masculinity and Sexuality in Modern Mexico*, ed. Víctor Macías-González and Anne Rubenstein (Albuquerque: University of New Mexico Press, 2012), pp. 101-31.

Blue Sunday

Moralists from
Yankee-landia
have started a
harsh campaign
against the vices
sapping body and soul.
They're so noble,
they've even
established a law
that no one may
set foot outside
one's home on Sundays,
unless they're
on their way to raise
saintly prayers,
sing sweet psalms,
because they're
squeaky clean,
as if bathed
with water and "lye,"
down to their souls.

No one will go
to the moving pictures,
no one will go
to the beaches,
no one will go
to the parks
without shame;
because the devil
sticks his tail
inside the movie houses
and steals souls;
sin sunbathes
on the beaches

and haunts the coffeehouses
where the "shimie"
and other lubricous
dances are danced;
and in the parks...
the crisp air gets
the girls all excited,
so that they feel
sweet and intimate urges,
while the elderly
men and women
relive blasts
from the past,
sheer joy, moments
that soothe them.

If anyone's eyes
should focus
on certain ladies'
curves, they're guilty
(for that's the age-
old law), and that gaze
will be fined
20 smackeroos.
Excuse me if I
use a metaphor
(it sounds more literary):
it's said that with
this new campaign,
of "Blue Sunday" —
as they call it here
in Holy Yankee-landia —
boy canaries
cannot cohabitate
with girl canaries;
for if they should kiss,

the wrathful saints
would unleash their ire
upon canary souls.

Poor canaries...!
They can't live in peace,
inside or out
of the cage...

Baseball Chronicles

Say what you will, but Mexicali
has won the second Series
of the Imperial Valley League;
up next, we have the final game,
which will prove to be a sensation.
With regards to the last game,
we must honorably confess
that the other team
played much better than ours;
if we won, well, that's
what Fate desired...
In the end, our sun-toasted players won
(yes, with unheard-of struggles),
with nine runs in the bottom half.
An act of God!

Ramírez and Pujol Terán
were brilliant. And especially
Caballito, "Ace" of the "Aces" of "Baseball,"
who slugged a home run
with such "bona sorte"
that the ball swooshed
past the stadium's clock,
taking the hour and minute hands
with it, and sped on for something
like 14 miles. A pleasant *gringo*
who played while squatting,
(an odd incident),
brimming with undue enthusiasm,
handed Cabal a five spot
with the noble intention
of taking Míster to the cleaners.
However, the "Chinacals,"
with embraces, kisses, shouts, and ovations,

and lacking any loose change,
celebrated a majestic play
by Cabal, aka "Califa."

A disagreeable incident transpired;
the gentlemen presiding as umpires
naturally didn't match the standards
of those from El Centro, California,
unlike the honorable folk
from their nation;
so they pulled a switcheroo
and called up some other guys
to replace those who judged
with "less impartiality."
But their struggles and ruses were to no avail:
nothing new occurred.

For those from El Centro,
taking on our heroic "Champion Cids,"
neither the change in umpires,
nor the replacement of pitchers,
nor the "Cabal-listic" and exterminating
swats of the colossal catcher
could help; nothing could silence
the thundering success of our players.

A good thing our determined champions
triumphed over their apathy
from yesteryear... for as some say,
this was due to the "Meat Wagon"... *

According to the prognosticators
out there, this week the "Chicagüenses"
will bat an explosive game
against the Mexicalenses —
one that will go down in history,
at least for residents of the Imperial.

The "Calcetines Blancos" of Chicago —
the "White Socks," as they say in *inglés* —
reign supreme in every "Baseball"
tournament played in the American Union,
and if they, these Supposed Masters, do
indeed arrive this week
to play against the *real* Masters,
our Místers,
we will have bragging rights,
and will shout loud in the streets!

We've got the best team in the Valley.
To each his own.

And here we finish this hasty
dish that's neither fragrant nor tasty.

* *An Ambulance.*

A Major Bust

The Honorable Police Inspector,
along with a few agents,
the type fortified with the purest
strain of intelligence,
who don't suffer from negligence
and never sleep, night or day,
made a major bust.
While stockpiling tips and taking precautions,
they found a certain den
where opium is consumed,
and they also caught, red-handed,
two Chinese tycoons,
very prominent
and piggish ones...
(here I ask my reader to spit)...
for the heroic agents
apprehended the magnates
as the two were puff-puff-puffing
from filthy pipes between their teeth.
And those two Mongols would still be there,
surrendering themselves to that
dirty vice — perhaps dreaming of Confucius
dancing the "shimmy" with Theda Bara —
if the Honorable Police Inspector
had not torn them from their reveries
and sent them to the slammer,
or, at the very least —
if I must tell the truth —
to the Hotel Cota.

In addition to the pipes,
word on the street is
the police found the following
in that Chinese hovel:
a thousand packets of low-quality,

regular, and extra fine opium,
as well as soft couches, combs,
brushes, and other items
used by those women
in skirts that reach down to their ankles.
Also found: a complete ledger
listing the profits made by some
secret society, whose name escapes me.
Another item: a guide
on how to cultivate poppies
and marijuana,
and a scheme to smuggle,
in broad daylight,
the dreamed-of drug,
without fearing a thing
from the spies in Customs.
This victorious blow
against the addicts
and dealers of that killer drug
proves they can no longer
get away with their crimes,
because they can't find palms to grease...
(I ask the readers to pardon that expression)...
This sets a good precedent
and is, naturally, an effective remedy
against pollution in our environment.

Good for the Police Inspector,
who doesn't view that vice
as a source of profit.
This is how things were done
"when God's will ruled the day"...

April 10, 1921
Mexicali, B.C.

According to some estimates, by 1920, the Chinese population of Mexicali — which had originally come to the Imperial Valley to build the irrigation system that supported its agricultural industry — outnumbered the native Mexican population 10 to one. The relations between the native Mexicans and Chinese were complicated and often tense, as this poem demonstrates. The Chinese were accused of spreading and profiting from the vices of gambling, opium smuggling, and prostitution. In reality, the community's contribution to the economic and cultural life of Mexicali is rich and long-lasting. The neighborhood in which the Chinese settled is called La Chinesca, and it is still home to some 5,000 Mexicans of Chinese descent. See James R. Curtis, "Mexicali's Chinatown," *Geographical Review* 85, no. 3 (July 1995), pp. 335-348; Robert H. Duncan, "The Chinese and the Economic Development of Northern Baja California, 1889-1929," *The Hispanic American Historical Review* 74, no. 4 (November 1994), pp. 615-647; Evelyn Hu-Dehart, "The Chinese of Baja California Norte, 1910-1934," *Proceedings of the Pacific Coast Council on Latin American Studies* 12 (San Diego: San Diego State University Press, 1986), pp. 9-30; and Julian Lim, "Chinos and Paisanos: Chinese Mexican Relations in the Borderlands," *Pacific Historical Review* 79, no. 1 (February 2010), pp. 50-85. For more context, see Jason Oliver Chang, *Chino: Anti-Chinese Racism in Mexico, 1880-1940* (Urbana: University of Illinois Press, 2017); Robert Chao Romero, *The Chinese in Mexico 1882-1940* (Tucson: University of Arizona Press, 2010); and Fredy González, *Paisanos Chinos: Transpacific Politics among Chinese Immigrants in Mexico* (Berkeley: University of California Press, 2017).

A Stormy Session at City Hall

During the "Honorable" session at City Hall
of this past Friday,
the leftist council members
put everything on the line,
with the aim of removing
the Mayor from office,
blaming him for the scourge
of opium and morphine,
which they said existed,
according to "the people."

I'm not going to waste
a single breath covering
so pitiful a scene: I wish only
to provide you with a sketch,
rendered in my own manner
but faithful to the events,
of how the Governing Councils
run things... quasi-autonomous...
I will give them a branding worthy
of those lacking scruples and morals.

The session's open for proceedings. It's five o'clock.
Not a single council member
is missing.
The Secretary reads
the Notes. His monotonous drone
is like the buzz of a fat
and sluggish fly.
Rosas ponders deeply; Chávez purrs
and then thinks for a bit;
Roncal snores; Ríos smiles
and half closes his eyes, as if
he were about to go fishing in outer space;
Rodríguez is sullen;

the public squirm in their seats,
but then the voice
of the Councilman being addressed resounds —
he politely asks
that certain phrases he never said
last Friday be lifted from the Notes;
he then proceeds to insult the Secretary
and Don Otto as well;
but upon hearing that the Notes
have been corrected, his rage
subsides. Now on to more important matters:
the slaughter of the (non-scape-)goat
that Don Golías carried out, and the hog
that Don Lolo executed;
trees clogging up the canals
belong to I-can't-remember-which *Rancho,*
and they're either growing over
or through the property line... Who gives a...!?
(I was trying to find a rhyme there,
but didn't even care *that* much.)
The ingots of silver
taken from some country bumpkin,
which he claims are no heavier
that his 15 offspring;
Iribe's resignation; and friendly
Pancho's appeal
for some "political clout" straight-
away — if we're not here for *that,*
then what's it all about?
On to the stipend provided for the Electoral Counsel
(a mere six pesos per day)
and other myriad matters, which they finish
addressing at 10:15 pm.
(And they say the councilmembers
aren't overpaid!)

Then, at last... the bell rings
for those who wish to inflict
some full-frontal slaps
against the poor working people
who suffer cuts in their wages
because of the economy,
which doesn't affect
the Mayor's lavish salary,
nor those of other politicos,
who know how to pocket
the spare change because...
well, that's their talent.
Private police agents
are suppressed from
the proceedings as well,
and after some discussion,
and some blows from a broom,
and a brilliant defense
of the Treasury,
come the storms,
the thunder and lightning,
and the raging rains
on the sterile plain —
that's how Lugo Rodríguez
lashed out against naïve Moller,
who, according to his allies,
is a stand-up guy.
Some say that law is sovereign;
that the 1917 Constitution
hasn't been finalized;
that Reyes is not a councilmember;
that they caught Manuel Díaz
taking care of illegal gamblers
under the guise of Security;
Moller who said that they used to say
he was of pure German blood;
But truth be told, our two councilmembers

didn't think he was up to snuff
to be Mayor, Moller just seems to parrot
our councilmembers, but he's brasher,
so that when they can't prove his words,
they have to discredit the judgments
of the Honorable Cabildo;
keep quiet, or the public will believe
that this is about another
cockfight arena being approved.

It was midnight on the dot
(as the saying goes)
when those attending
at last hit the hay.

God willing, those readers
who have reached this point
won't send me
straight to hell.

May 1921
Mexicali, B.C.

A Resounding Victory

To extol the posthumous victory
obtained by our team
in the League's closing game,
O Muse of Baseball, sing through me!
Give me the divine inspiration
of immortal Homer!
Lend me the trumpets of Fame
to inform the whole world
that no game in the Imperial Valley
could pull the wool over a Mexican's eyes;
that despite the tricks and scams
committed by the umpires,
despite the fact that our ballplayers
are so ugly, so dark
(I don't say this because of Buiti or Corúa,
even less because of Agapito),
they clinched the win. And now I reach out
to those from Mexicali as well as those from El Centro.
Now that the struggle's over,
as good neighbors and sharecroppers,
Join hands and proclaim:
Bravo for Mexicali! Long live El Centro!

The game's about to begin. There's a great
number of spectators on the bleachers,
and there are more than 400 cars.

Out of respect for the Regulation,
our team bats first;
the opposing team rolls up their sleeves.
The "pitcher" is on his mound.
The "catcher" and the "ump"
have donned their armor.
Buiti is up "at bat," and the Mexicalenses
chatter away...

First inning: one point for Mexicali.
Second: a run for El Centro.
Third: head to head.
And then nothing... It's like a cemetery out there,
until the sixth inning, when the opposing team
adds another point to our score.

Neither of the two teams
gets anything done during their next encounter.
During the eighth, nothing for Mexicali,
but El Centro gets another run.
It's three to two, and our neighbors
are winning; our boys
will play for all or nothing
in the ninth inning.

Faces turn pale. Our "paisanos"
hold their breath in the stands,
and if silence had wings,
one could hear them flutter.

El Corúa goes up to bat — and crack!
He connects and reaches first base.
Then Ramírez follows the example
of his teammate, and finds
himself just as lucky.

Next is Terán. Three balls, two "strikes,"
and then a solid hit —
he makes it to second base,
and the others make it safely home.
Buitti's up at bat — watch out!
He's a real slugger!

The pitcher throws the ball,
and with the force a cloud uses

to unleash a lightning bolt, Buiti
hits the ball and… "homerun"!

All of our compatriots
stand up and shout,
applaud and jump,
throw their hats in the air.

Some spring down to the diamond, hug Buiti,
While others sob and kiss the afternoon's Colossus.
All the while, one of them
collects some dollars,
around 40 bucks,
which he offers to the shortstop
as a token of admiration and affection.
A certain Míster, overtaken by enthusiasm,
gives him five pesos.
Then the excitement subsides
and the game continues:
two more points for the winners,
and zero for their adversaries.

A recap: six runs for Mexicali,
only three for El Centro.

Here we have burned a lot of incense
for Buiti, while Terán was forgotten —
but he was responsible
for the points earned by Ramírez and Corúa,
which clinched the victory,
not to mention Buitemea's homerun,
a true merit.

As always, Agapito was formidable;
focused, guarding third base,
catching balls way up in the clouds.
Ramírez played wonderfully.

The fielders, good as usual...
Terancito and Aresenio proved
worthy of *novenas* honoring
saints now in heaven.

The umpires were quite partial;
they didn't call foul when one of their own
was wrong, which isn't a surprise...
They were at home.
El Examiner noted that this
was the first time a foreign country
had won the championship.

Olé for the little Indians!
What an honor for Mexico...!

April 1921
Mexicali, B.C.

Neighbors of Mexicali

The neighbors of Mexicali insist
that Señor Governor Lugo's
two most recent projects
don't pass the smell test.
The first one is meant
to improve the spurious
water service, which we know
amounts to zilch;
for example, some neighborhoods
have no water access because
the pipes don't work,
and the pressure is weak,
and the weather in those areas
scalds. For the project to amount
to more than just words,
(unlike many others proposed
by other governors at other times),
Señor Lugo exhibited the cost of
a tank holding a hundred thousand gallons,
and he was able to sign the contract
without overspending.
The other project in question
is for a power plant; as it stands,
people suffer from bad, costly service,
because, Jesus!, the businessmen
only wish to line their pockets;
they rob the people and... See ya!
Well, now we've requested estimates,
from both abroad and at home,
on an equitable basis,
and the project will be carried out
by the company that charges least,
and treats a Mexican fairly.
Because, really, we've already got
water and power in Mexicali

without having to rely on Calexico,
which kindly offers those services
in exchange for our hard-earned money...
At last, we will witness the fulfillment
of those election promises
about water and power and cheap land,
offered to the people so many times
just to seize power.
Look, all of you: frankly,
like a decent Mexican, I am overjoyed
by the better infrastructure
that I leave outlined above,
but my heart breaks
when I consider the scheming
of the parasitical and pathetic politicians
as they try to benefit from the spending;
so thanks to Governor Lugo
who'll provide water and power for all.

June 1922
Mexicali, B.C.

José Inocente Lugo (1871-1963) was a prominent Mexican politician who served as Governor of the Northern District of Baja
California from 1922 to 1923.

Carnival in Mexicali

The Carnival has started
under favorable auspices,
and no there's no doubt
it will prove to be
a sumptuous and splendid event,
even more than in the past,
thanks to the efforts
of the ladies who make up
the Great Organizing
Committee of Festivals.
They have organized
soirées that really proved
to be beautiful
social parties,
and now the contest
for the next Carnival Queen
has begun;
the divine Belem Vega
has earned 500 votes,
while Elena Urroz,
(a celestial houri),
has received 150;
we hope the suffrages
will exceed a hundred thousand.
The enthusiasm surrounding
the contest for the crown
has reached a barbaric pitch.
And now Don Víctor Carusso,
the Rajah of splendidness himself,
has said that he will personally
place the royal crown
on the most popular head —
and he's as good as his word
(so let's see, let's see).
The Committee is composed

of the most distinguished little
ladies, and from the upper crust
of Mexicali-Calexico society,
and is bravely directed
by Laurita R. De Ulloa,
who hasn't rested, laboring
to make sure the future parties
of the Carnival will make a
splash on the society pages.
Very shortly, we will publish
the effigy of the Beauty
who has received the most
suffrages by Saturday,
along with a list of the candidates
(a rosebush in full bloom)
who will remain in this royal contest,
until the very end.

February 1923
Mexicali, B.C.

Victor Carusso (d. 1946) was an El Paso businessman who grew
rich selling goods to Mexican revolutionaries. He and his family
moved to San Francisco in 1923.

The Elections

The elections for the very
Illustrious City Council
have come and gone,
like flickers across
the silver screen: in silence.
There were some "protestors"
against the indignant acts
that the parties flung
in each other's faces:
how some voter-registrations
were denied to conscientious
citizens from three or four
districts, because they didn't
belong to the "circuit,"
while, on the other hand,
in other areas,
even children got to vote.

The results: according
to the "Reds and Farmers Party,"
they emerged triumphant,
while those from the other party,
the "National Club of the People,"
assure us they won as well.

We'll see how this mess
ends at the meeting
of the Honorable City Council
on the first day of the year.

At the Eden

The revue *Arte Nuevo*,
made by Chacel,
debuts this Sunday
at the Eden;
it features a cast
that... only he knows how
to make it work so well...
There's Ernesto Rubio,
a stupendous tenor,
one of those who move
the entire theater,
from the foundations
to the ceiling
(if that's not true, let
our Eden say so).
Also featured is Teté Tapia —
the divine Esther —
an actress who marches
with art and faith
towards God's Glory.
Bravos for Teté!
And Beautiful Carmela,
the flutter of whose feet
makes the angels —
and even St. Joseph —
gaze down from heaven
and shout *Olé!*

And up next
is Señora Areu,
who embodies
the roles she plays;
and the young lady,
Señorita Chacel,

an artist's delight,
nothing more can be said.

In terms of the masculine
element, three stand out
in particular:
Chacel himself
(of course... he's the Director!),
Molgosa, and Pepet,
all of them veterans
of acting...

And we've not forgotten
about the chorus:
three gals and two guys,
and as one can see,
with a chorus like that,
you won't get much
of a "catchy" tune.
Rubio, the tenor,
is weak at vocalization,
and at times he's too big
for his britches.

And... excuse me...
but the lovely Té-Té —
how her treble warbles;
still, that's not her
strength; I said it once,
and I'll say it again:
the Glory that awaits her
is the same spiral staircase
that Sarah Bernhardt
and a hundred other
world famous actresses
are fated to ascend.
Did I say that well?

That's enough for today.
In a bit, I will happily
busy myself
with the Modern Revue
made by Chacel.

December 13, 1922
Mexicali, B.C.

Míster BLIND

Bernal is likely reporting on a performance by the Compañía de Arte Nuevo, directed by Arturo Chacel (b. 1877), a Cuban-born playwright and social activist who became the "Supreme Organizer" of La Liga Protectora Latina in the United States. Areu was the maiden name of Chacel's wife, Angela (b. 1876); their daughter, Angelica Chacel (1908-1990), was a singer and artist. See Nicolás Kanellos, *A History of Hispanic Theatre in the United States: Origins to 1940* (Austin: University of Texas Press, 1990), pp. 24, 30, 68, and 209n38; F. Arturo Rosales, *Chicano! The History of the Mexican American Civil Rights Movement* (Houston, TX: Arte Público Press, 1997), p. 63; and *idem*, *¡Pobre Raza!: Violence, Justice, and Mobilization among México Lindo Immigrants, 1900-1936* (Austin: University of Texas Press, 1999), p. 28.

A recording featuring Angelica Chacel, "Hermanos Areu," and Beatriz Noloesca (1903-1979), originally issued on the Brunswick label in 1926, has been digitized by the Arhoolie Foundation's Strachwitz Frontera Collection of Mexican and Mexican American Recording: http://frontera.library.ucla.edu/artists/beatriz-noloesca-angelica-chacel-y-hermanos-areu

Pact of Silence

The illustrious members
of the Governing Council,
using their saintly right,
in full authority,

signed a pact
that covers everything:
from "souvenirs"
for one's family

to the very traditional
"don't you say a word."
And they call the pact
a "Pact of Honor,"

which obliges them
to use it only in a moral manner,
and prudently,
during their meetings.

So. Rosas and Castro,
as usual, are at
each other's throats,
getting worked up?

Immediately,
with a lofty gesture,
Loera reminds them
of that signed pact.

So. Ángeles and Mérida
are clashing? During their scene,
a fellow member
reminds them of the pact.

And in such a plain
and simple manner,
the Honorable Sirs
march on towards wonders,

without my discovering
whether all this was done
as a pretext to cover
up some scandals...

Nor did the members
set aside their old squabbles,
because they fear
a whipping from

Big Daddy Government,
for the order implies
that if people rise up,
they too get the belt.

One needs to send
a letter of kudos
to those council members
for their conversion...

Let's hope none of this
will make one think:
they're robbing Peter
to pay Paul...

While Paul
was looking elsewhere...

March 1923
Mexicali, B.C.

Míster BLIND

The Filibusters

The Filibusters
from behind the fence
are lamenting
their piggish behavior,
which has led them
down darkened paths.
How I pity
the Filibusters!...

Poor lil' orphans!
And though it may sting,
we must tell them
they have no mother;
and if they still have one...
that unhappy woman!
Would to God
they had been stillborn!

Branded
treacherous & cunning...
How I pity
the Filibusters!...

And if hunger
should lead them to treason,
then I'd take
even greater pity...
Poor saps! Egged on
by the "Big Bosses,"
who see them
as a bunch of putzes,
vile instruments
of their perfidious
work, while they
live high on the hog;

pitiful Judases,
going for chump change...
How I pity
the Filibusters!...

They dreamt of invading
the Northern District,
but they lacked "passports"...
and now they bewail
their failure in a foreign
lexicon. Poor saps!
Held in contempt
throughout Calexico,
even by foreigners.
How I pity
the Filibusters!...

October 1922
Mexicali, B.C.

The so-called "Filibusters" were supporters of Colonel Esteban Cantú, Governor of the Northern District of Baja California from 1915 to 1920. They wished to return him to power and were gathering arms in California while being watched by Revolutionary troops on the Mexican side of the border.

Wide-Open City

At the first spark
of Dawn
I left Mexicali
for Tijuana
via the shortest route:
through the mountain range.
The trip takes less
than half a day,
and that's if it's
a smooth one, if
you're lucky — as long
as Death doesn't show
her silhouette
in the ravines
that line the road
on either side,
in whose black depths
one glimpses cars
shattered to smithereens,
along with drivers and passengers.

San Diego! Beautiful port!
The twin of any
city in the United
States. Frozen,
with its extra-high-rise
hotels, parks, streetcars
and asphalt,
and its numbered streets:
the main one's
called Main,
and its storefronts
are the same

as in all other cities:
"Kress," "Sole Service,"
and the "Five and Dime."

The next morning,
I left San Diego
and arrived at Tijuana,
quickly, really quickly, as my foot
pressed on the Lil' Ford's gas pedal,
and in a half-hour I found
myself in the Cosmo-
Metropolis of Sin;
two blocks full of whorehouses
and cantinas
and cabarets, to which
the Messalinas of a thousand arts
lure their clients,
while dancing in scanty attire,
drinking, and flirting
with the rubes
who fall into their nets.
(If you're ignorant of the facts,
seek them out for yourself).
Saturdays and Sundays
are a sight:
"gringos" clog the streets,
each with his own
escort; the gringos feign
they're temperate, that they're
just engaging in polite
conversation with the natives,
while they sip their
"innocent" cocktails
until rosy-fingered dawn
piously spreads
across Tijuana.

The curious tourist
just here to study
the local customs,
who lacks the scratch
to paint the town red
will hit the hay early,
but all in vain!
As soon as his first snore erupts,
he's awakened by a brutal
banging on his door...
Some Míster slurring,
"Open up, Juanita",
And you, dear Sir,
lose your cool,
you roar, you rage,
but a simple "*Excuse me*"
from that intruder
calms you down.
Lord! What abuse!...
You fall back asleep
and then, through the wall,
you hear a woman's voice
shriek: "You jerk!"
followed by a slam.
You peek out your door
and see a man
leave without his coat...
At last, round about
four in the morning,
things quiet down,
you catch some shuteye,
when, all of a sudden...
What luck!...
Two cats fall in love
on a nearby rooftop!...
For the rest, Tijuana —
open city,

open door to Sin
and an easy buck,
which funds the Treasury
well, very well —
can't afford water or sidewalks,
electricity or pavement,
sewage systems or signs...
It can't afford squat!
Because all the money
goes straight to Ensenada
and gets divvied up
"in a certain manner,"
so that in Tijuana,
they sing "La firulera" to that city...

July 11, 1921
Tijuana, B.C.

Let's Save Our Brother from the Hangman

There's a fellow countryman
at the foot of the gallows.
a brother of ours
who was forced to kill
one cursed moment
in self-defense.
The incident:
Aureliano Pompa,
young migrant
from Sonora,
seeking work in
this Babylon;
like other gullible ones,
he believed the tall
tales of good wages
and shorter
work days, among
other pipe dreams.

A foreigner to both language
and landscape,
the only work he found:
the back-breaking chores
of a peon. With determination,
he labored, faced myriad
ups and downs,
but, in the end, he never
achieved his deepest
dream, his hope:
to send back home
some dollars —
a cloth of tears
for his anguish.
Then... across the life of
Aureliano Pompa

proceeds a Red March:
our countryman
suffers an insult —
a foreman strikes him
in the face; again
and again,
they insult him,
and finally
they raise
a sledgehammer,
in threat.
Well, Pompa
steps back, pulls
out his pistol,
fires and kills
in self-defense.
That's how the witnesses,
who were not too few,
reported the incident:
and yet, Justice wishes
to see Pompa swing
from the gallows.

First *El Heraldo*,
then the rest
of the press (let's say,
in the name of Justice),
have started a fund
to save him, asking
for contributions
from our countrymen.
Several lawyers
have taken on the case,
and have fought
valiantly to spare
Aureliano Pompa's life.
Let us all help, however

we can, in this
noble endeavor:
to save our brother,
our countryman,
who now awaits his final
hour in a jail cell,
from the hangman.

Save a poor mother,
from martyrdom
as she silently sobs
and sighs
for her absent son;
she feels her own neck
snap in the noose
as she thinks of her son,
(Lady of Sorrows!);
she may even miss
the consolation
of a kiss
before his final hour...

LET US ALL HELP
AURELIANO POMPA.

March 31, 1923
Mexicali, B.C.

In March 1923, Aurelio Pompa, a cement worker born in Sonora and residing in Los Angeles, was sentenced to death for the murder of William Donaldson McCue, a carpenter and veteran of the First World War, which occurred on October 19, 1922. Pompa was 21 years old when the sentence was handed down. According to the prosecution, Pompa shot McCue, his foreman at a job site, after the two quarreled over a tool. According to Pompa, McCue, who had already beaten him earlier in the day, accosted him after the argument, and he fired in self-defense. The death sentence was affirmed by the California Supreme Court in November 1923. A petition for clemency was signed by some 13,000 people, and Mexico's president, Álvaro Obregón, sent a personal plea, but California's Governor, Friend Richardson (1865-1943), found no cause to commute the sentence. Pompa was hanged at San Quentin on March 7, 1924. Pompa's fate sparked outrage in the Mexican-American community and inspired a popular corrido, "Vida, Proceso, y Muerte de Aurelio Pompa" ("The Life, Trial, and Death of Aurelio Pompa"). See *Edward J. Escobar, Race, Police, and the Making of a Political Identity: Mexican Americans and the Los Angeles Police Department*, 1900-1945 (Berkeley: University of California Press, 1999), pp. 138-39; *Julie Leininger Pycior, Democratic Renewal and the Mutual Aid Legacy of US Mexicans* (College Station: Texas A&M University Press, 2014), pp. 59-60; and *F. Arturo Rosales, ¡Pobre Raza!: Violence, Justice, and Mobilization among México Lindo Immigrants, 1900-1936* (Austin: University of Texas Press, 1999), pp. 150-51.

PART III

The Bullfight

According to
the opinions I credit,
last Sunday's bullfight
was quite acceptable,
especially when one considers
that the cattle arrived
haggard from the road's rough
conditions, yet were still
able to fulfill their destiny...
The public's darlings: Torquito
and Rivera, at the height of their fame;
the first one started,
the second one followed;
they both made little use
of the cape and *banderillas*.
Torquito wielded his *muleta*
with ease and worked wonders
with his sword;
he finished off the first bull and
the third with one stab,
(one by one, course),
in the precise spot.
Rivera, wielding the instruments
of Death against the second bull,
had no such luck,
because of the bull himself —
he moved from one side to the other —
and he could only inflict
a few pricks
upon that half-bull —
some punctures, some scratches;
finally, approaching the animal,
he struck a furious blow,
so that the beast
went to the next world

with a "horrible phrase"
on the fleshy part of its neck.
But right when the *mulillero* comes out
and drags away the ruminant,
the bull pen opens
and there appears — arrogant,
and with enough strength
to charge at the entire universe —
the last of the horned animals,
which, in its beauty, came first.
The crowd cheers the wild animal;
Pérez Rivera executes
the florid movements of his cape —
"veronicas" worthy of a hundred
thousand chronicles —
and Torquito stretches his frame,
flutters his cape, regaling us
with the best of the best.
The enemy is enshrouded
in the folds of the cape, and Torquito caresses
his horns. Reveilles shower down upon him
as he walks through the flower-fall,
among trumpet blasts, shouts, ovations,
which both of the bullfighters hear,
as they see caps and sombreros
(even a firefighter's kepi)
fall with cigars, cigarettes, hard candy, coins...
The *banderillas* repeat the act;
it seems as if the those two
skillful individuals have made a pact
to show off their daring do;
first, two from Rivera,
of which the Great Belmonte would be proud,
then one from Toquita,
which proves to be even better,
just like the Great Gaona!
(That comparison is called for!)

They play at death; Pérez Rivera
grabs the red cape. A natural pass,
another sweep of the cape, though lower,
and another across the animal;
one at its chest; one at the knees...
Amazing! The young matador keeps only
the smallest distance, and toys with his
own life right in front of the bull's snout!
But the moment comes when the bull
pays dearly for its bravery
and rare caprice,
for showing off its beautiful frame.
The boy unsheathes his sword,
takes aim, a prick, and... a death blow!
While the iron's hot! A new step; he flexes
his arm... the sword is driven hilt-deep!
The battered bull loses control,
crumbles to the sand, decimated,
dead from its giant head to its tail!...
And in case it still has some breath left,
Rivera delivers the coup de grâce.
The musicians, the public, and... the bulls
that, from the corral, hear the din
and guess at their fate,
embrace, shout, and roar
at the death of the other bull,
(to each his own "idiom," one wisely warns),
while the very sun, as a Spaniard put it,
suspends its course and weeps
with joy at the sight of Rivera.
as if he were its own child.
(And of course, since the Sun is the King of Heaven,
it must be Iberian.)
El Carbonero Grande and El Goanita
did well; Limeño perfomed
at a high level.
The lance... no need of that!

The ticket sales: good for seats in the sun,
worse for those in the shade.
The public: satisfied.
And that's where the story ends.
Period.

March 1923
Mexicali, B.C.

The Cartepillar
(The Worm of Venice)

In Venice Beach,
as in the rest of the world's
tourist shores, we find
an immense variety
of fun spots. Each year
those who set up rides
bring something new for the public,
who make a mass pilgrimage
to the sweet attractions
of a "*gud taim*,"
or to bask in the caresses
and smile of the sea.

This very summer
we find, apart from the usual
rollercoaster, "House
of Madness," the infernal
path between the baskets
that rattle one's body
and might have been designed
by Satan himself, as well as
the racecourse where we see
grown men among
the little girls,
astride "Sam" or
"John" (the horses
bear those names and others),
and those charming creatures,
"Amazonians of Perfection"...
whose flagrancy flutters in the wind
like a triumphant banner...
In addition to all these
places for entertainment
(they are many others,

but, for now, let's speak
of a most original one):
 the gigantic "Cartepillar"
(Worm), ("cartepilar"
to spell it like a *pocho*),
whose passengers ride
in comfortable cars.
Said animal
is circular in shape,
with a diameter of some fifteen
feet, more or less,
and it loops around, thanks
to the sorcery
of a special mechanism.
Hoping to study this rare
"cartepilar" from within,
I approached the animal,
with many others,
and placed myself beside
(ever so cleverly),
a pretty lil' countrywoman
from "these parts."

The worm lurches forward
in its irregular shape,
and while it runs, it cloaks us,
little by little, in its vast
carapace — if one can speak freely —
truly imitating
a gigantic worm
on its circular route,
and leaving us
in absolute darkness,
behind thick curtains
(Virgin of Soledad!)
that separate each car;

and a rough wind
from beneath blows upwards
with insistent cruelty...

The illusion doesn't last long...
The speed of this ringed
vehicle slows,
the carapace gradually
rises, and...
Let's stop with the details.

I say farewell to my lady
in a special manner,
and get out and stumble
into an acquaintance;
he whispers to me
in a confidential tone:
now that you use lipstick,
be careful, 'cause you got
some on your nose,
hombre — unbecoming...
(This could happen even to a dead man
on the "cartepillar.")

Readers, now you've heard
the latest news
of what happens to couples
who seek a grand "*gud taim.*"

June 1923
Los Angeles, Calif.

Míster BLIND

In Defense of Phillips

This Friday, they brought back
from Tegucigalpa
Clara Phillips,
the most evil woman
the world has seen
since the start of Christendom...
All condemn her,
all mistreat her
in their hearts,
all throw mountains
of hate at her,
especially those ladies
who beg for Justice
yet cry for Vengeance.
No one has any pity
for this wretch,
who loved deliriously,
who felt the deadly gust
of black jealousy.
She saw they were robbing her
of his immense affection,
and as those Soul-Thieves
have no law against them,
she, driven mad
by this disgrace,
roared like a tigress
deprived of her cubs,
and bared her claws.
Who is so cynical
as to render
a simple verdict?
How would they dare?
Do they stick their tongue

out at Justice?
Imagine the battles
that grip her soul!...

I don't pardon the crime:
Human Justice
must correct it;
if they left it unpunished,
it would probably
be a worse disgrace.
But is it truly
possible for Man,
ignorant of the infinite
Mysteries of the soul,
armed only with "Codes,"
to judge one who kills?

June 1923
Mexicali, B.C.

Míster BLIND

On July 12, 1922, Clara Phillips, a former chorus girl, committed a sensational crime — the murder of her husband's lover,
Alberta Meadows, with a 15-cent hammer. The brutality of
the assault inspired the press to dub Phillips "Tiger Girl" and
"Tiger Woman." The day after the murder, Phillips's husband
went to the police; she was soon apprehended, tried, and con-
victed of second-degree murder. On December 5, 1922, she escaped from jail and remained a fugitive for four months, before
being caught in Tegucigalpa, Honduras. She was extradited to
California, served her term San in Quentin, and was released
on parole in 1935. See Joan Renner, "How Murderess Clara
Phillips Became 'Tiger Girl,'" *Los Angeles Magazine* (June 24,
2013): http://www.lamag.com/citythinkblog/how-murderess-
clara-phillips-became-tiger-girl/

Divorce

Unlike those from other places,
the people in this progressive
and hard-working county,
where everything is translated
into more gold, do not
regard holy matrimony,
that rope that binds souls together,
as a matter of "saecula saeculorum."
Here, sweet conjugality
is like any other business,
with honorable exceptions,
as everything must be.

The pretenders agree
to see the Judge, and without
any other preliminary
conditions, they finalize
the marriage like partners
signing a company contract.

What if things go south?
That's to say, the wedded couple
doesn't agree on things? The business
is liquidated in two shakes,
or, in other words: both
agree to a divorce.

The causes for untying
the conjugal knot
are infinite, thanks
to the legality of divorce.
Most often, it's women
who file for it. Hubby
sneezes too much
at night? The horror!

Cause to see the Judge
about a divorce.

Did the woman, on a whim,
get a lil' doggy, and the other,
I mean, the husband,
can't tolerate the yapping
that the mongrel unleashes
at every step? Well… ask for a divorce.
Does some schmuck of a husband
buy a "very luxurious"
hat for two pesos,
without his wife's permission?
What compliments he'll receive
for splurging and hiding!
You spent two whole pesos
on a hat?! That's it!
Then the refrain:
"Let's get a divorce."

Other couples separate
because the guy doesn't
meet expectations,
doesn't match up
to his wife's whims:
might as well get a divorce.
find someone more appetizing.

Luckily, the law,
does impose some limits
on the causes for divorce,
in the name of morality,
and certain ladies work
with admirable zeal
to "sanitize" the environment,
to foster more love in the home,
more respect for matrimony.

In order to assist
this noble undertaking —
since the fad for "records"
is at its height —
I propose a new survey:
THE SURVEY OF LASTING
MARRIAGE. First Prize goes
to the pair with the most kids.

June 1923
Los Angeles, Calif.

The Presidential Succession

Our politicians
are already preparing
for the upcoming
presidential election:
they've lived through three
or more of these,
and yet no party
has backed a candidate.
Why is that?
Some clamor for
General Calles,
(truth be told,
they're the majority),
while others root
for capable Huerta,
very honorable,
very popular,
but he himself says,
without hesitation,
from down in Hermosillo,
that he won't run.
The Agrarians clamor
for the radical
Soto y Gama;
all the teachers
side with Vasconcelos.
And the rest?
The clerics
won't show
their hand
but they scheme
without cease
to enforce
their will,
and so

they will gather
in the metropolis,
but they won't get
what they desperately want.
The reactionaries also
aim to rip out some nails,
And they already
have their candidate:
General
Don Félix Díaz,
who will run
(not the slightest
chance of him winning)
as a hopeful
(yet again?)
in the presidential
election.

No party
has talked trash,
each has launched
with gusto
into the campaign
in a way that's
frank and loyal,
and I must rectify:
in Mexicali,
the National
Cooperativists
have appointed
their candidate:
General Calles —
a man who will,
without a doubt,
in the eyes
of Míster Blind
and of all

good liberals,
carry forth
the patriotic work
of our current Leader.

June 1923
Los Angeles, Calif.

Míster BLIND

Plutarco Elías Calles (1877-1945) won the 1924 election and became the 40th President of Mexico, succeeding Álvaro Obregón. Like Obregón, he was supported by the Mexican Laborist Party (*Partido Laborista Mexicano*, PLM), in coalition with a number of others, including the National Cooperativist Party (*Partido Nacional Cooperativista*, PNC). Adolfo de la Huerta, a former ally of Obregón and Calles, revolted against them in 1923, but he was defeated and fled to Los Angeles in March 1924. Antonio Diaz Soto y Gama (1880-1967) was the founder and leader of the National Agrarian Party (*Partido Nacional Agrarista*, PNA); he did not run against Calles. José Vasconcelos (1882-1959) was a well-known intellectual who theorized of the Mexican "cosmic race" (*la raza cósmica*). Vasconcelos served as the Secretary of Public Education under Obregón; he opposed Calles and resigned in 1924, but continued to advocate for educational reform.

Mexico in Caricature

In a theater on Broadway
"the name of which I have
no desire to recall," our beloved
Mexico is being denigrated.
The grotesque absurdity
is entitled *On the Border*,
with a cast of three
or four shameless idiots,
written with the claws
of one those "soaks"
who cross our border
because their native land is dry,
and in cabarets and cantinas
bursting with foreigners,
they observe Blue Sundays...
They toast Bacchus and Venus,
then come home
and disparage us.

On the stage there appears
the Calexico border crossing
in front of Mexicali
(judging, at least,
by the number of cantinas
facing each other
across the international "line") .
The well-known crossroads:
"United States" on one side,
and on the other, "Mexico."

Someone supposed to be
one of our Heads of Security
walks onto the stage
(an honorable citizen,
one of us, authentic),

peacocking in a green
leather coat, with a white
vest, and red pants —
in other words: Mexico.
A "charro" sombrero, and two
rifles slung over his shoulder,
and a dagger at his side.
If I could have set off
an explosion, both playwright
and protagonist would have
been blown to smithereens.

And then come other scenes,
turning our indignation
from red to black, scenes that
I won't describe out of respect
for the public who reads this.

God willing, the Consul of Mexico
assigned to this city
finds out about the case
and sets things right.
Until then, the Mexican colony,
as well as the citizens of
Hispano-America, should not
patronize an establishment
that denigrates what is ours,
intending to violate
the most sacred codes
and honor of a free people
deserving all due respect
from the largest, most cultured
country in the Universe.

May 1923
Los Angeles, Calif.

Míster BLIND

The quoted phrase in the second and third lines occurs in the opening sentence of the first chapter of Miguel de Cervantes's *Don Quixote* (1605-15).

México Auténtico

Debuting at the Auditorium,
that most elegant among
the finest venues in the city
of Los Angeles (it's not
by chance it's the top
choice of the Stars),
is the spectacle *México Auténtico*,
brought to us by Nelly Fernández:
a very Mexican production,
featuring artists of pure blood,
whose motto is: "*For the* Raza,
for the Homeland, and for Art."

The Mexican press
and the Yankee newspapers
have already praised
our countrymen; but before
they continue their tour
to Europe, allow me
to dedicate these poor "stabs
in the dark" to them,
from the heart.

Maestro Cantú initiates
the evening program
with his wise baton,
conducting "Aires Nacionales,"
that vernacular music
which evokes the tribulations
of a *Raza* of Titans
in its divine language.
Nelly, graceful Nelly,
an admirable vocalist
whose songs let us delight
in the breezes of our valleys

and the diamantine dew
upon the roses;
Nelly, the soul of the "troupe":
Youth, Beauty, and Art...
She performs a few folk dances
(among them "El Jarabe
Tapatío" and "La Sandunga")
in an appropriate costume,
executing the scene
with inimitable mastery.

Isabel Zenteno sings,
and her warm, smooth voice,
the voice of a dramatic soprano,
with sweetest sonorities,
makes us feel, to our cores,
the national ballads.

"El que calla otorga." A poem
by Don Ernesto Finance,
recited by the author himself,
while wearing the typical costume
of a farmer among the *chinampas*.
In his picturesque phrases,
he tells us how impatiently
our *Patria* awaits our return;
brimming with tenderness,
he delivers us a sweet message
from that beloved land
with green magueys
and white lilies
and red tulips —
he speaks of the florid
chinampas, the great sentries
with their great peaks
that guard the valley,
and the beautiful twilights

that bathe in the sun's blood,
and those full-moon nights,
that prove indelible.
This most tender of monologues
lifts and carries us, ever so briefly,
on the wings of a Dream,
towards our dear *Patria*.

And then comes the Cuban dance
(the work of Nelly Fernández
and Rafael Díaz). With each step,
both reveal to us elegant
sensuousness.
In the foxtrot, Nelly stands out;
rich silks enfold
her sculptural forms,
which radiate Light and Harmony,
Youth, Beauty, and Art.

Four little Mexican women
dancing gracefully
complement the ensemble:
small of foot, vast of soul,
eyes black as obsidian,
and lips like coral.
Another four beauties,
whom one would like to "lasso,"
make up the chorus:
almost a choir of angels...

Lovely decorations
depict enchanting landscapes
like Chapultepec, Xochimilco,
"The Desert," "The Volcanos"...

Let these poor lines go forth,
a humble homage,

full of love and admiration
for the great artists who work
their hearts out *"For the* Raza,
for the Homeland, and for Art."

June 1923
Los Angeles, Calif.

Míster BLIND

On Thursday, July 12, 1923, a critic for the *Los Angeles Times* reviewed a performance by "Nelly Fernandez and her company of all-Mexican singers and dancers" at the now-demolished Philharmonic Auditorium, which stood at 427 W. 5th St. The reviewer laments that the venue "was only half filled":

> The Mexican colony, even, is not turning out as it should, to say nothing of the Americans who have lived in Mexico or those who have not, who might like to see what Mexican singing and dancing and Mexican dress really are like, for most of the so-called such is no more Mexican than is chili con carne, that well-known Mexican dish, never heard of below the border.

The troupe is, according to the reviewer, the "first first-class Mexican company to come to the States in recent years," and the 21-year-old star is "more than 'simpatica.' She is 'chula,' which is more properly Mexican." We also learn that the manager "has given up Revolution for Art":

> He used to be a captain of a Mexican gunboat, and a cavalry officer under Villa. He is quite military about his stage work, and when he cries, "Todo el mundo adentro," one would think he was preparing an attack on a pueblo, or an hacienda at least.

"Singing Songs of Mexico," *Los Angeles Times*, 12 July 1923: 26.

PALOS DE CIEGO

Sin Padrino

A este libro le pasó lo que a esas criaturas que nacen entre la vida y la muerte, y que, a falta del padrino, son bautizadas por el progenitor, es decir: les echa éste el agua para que no vayan a ser un problema entre los billones de inmigrantes del Limbo...

El bautizo en este caso, es el prólogo, y el padrino, un dilecto amigo y atildado escritor, quien, por apuraciones de última hora, tal vez no tuvo tiempo de cumplir con ese cristiano deber.

Y en tan apurado trance; con los tres mil ejemplares del libro listos para su encuadernación, y en vísperas de salir para tierras de México, me he puesto a emborrachar cuartillas, a fin de decirle al "paciente" lector que disimule la mala catadura de la obra, la cual, como en el epigrama de Moratín: " lo mejor que tiene es la figura" ; y después de andar y desandar el camino trillado por todos los prologuistas, me he quedado en el mismo; díganlo si no, las siguientes líneas, que aquí estampo, solamente para cumplir con la fórmula establecida; ya que, con prólogo o sin él, lo bueno y malo del libro, sabrá apreciarlo igualmente el sensato lector.

Allá va, pues, la disculpa de rigor.

Palos de ciego he titulado a este libro, porque sus páginas fueron escritas apresuradamente, sin orden ni concierto, como destinadas a llenar la labor cuotidiana de un periódico; título que bien podrían aplicarse a cuantos asuntos de actualidad trata el moderno diarismo, pues los redactores tienen que incubar sus ideas al calor del tópico del momento, y bajo la tensión nerviosa que producen los linotipos pidiendo "copia", o bien, implorando a las rebeldes Musas que se han declarado en huelga cansadas de dar a luz...

En fin, aquí quedan estos pobres palos míos: recíbalos el lector a sabiendas de lo que son: toscos leños cortados al azar, que no sirviendo para otra cosa, quizá sirvan para combustible, y así se purifiquen de todo pecado. Amén.

Agosto de 1923
Los Angeles, Calif.

Míster BLIND
(Facundo Bernal)

PRIMERA PARTE

"La Prensa". Diario de la tarde

LA PRENSA se ha transformado
De la noche a la mañana
En diario bien informado;
Buena sorpresa ha llevado
La colonia mexicana,
Y con ella, es natural,
Toda la de habla española,
Que nos honra por igual
Leyéndonos, por lo cual
La nuestra no fue ella sola.
   Sin decirnos ¡agua va!
Se viene de sopetón
La Prensa; y es diario ya:
Si lo dudan, ¡aquí está
Nuestra primera edición!
Y aunque la verdad no es justo
"agarrarnos" de sorpresa,
Hay que perdonar el susto
Al enterarnos con gusto
¡que es verdad tanta belleza!
   Sí, señores, ¡somos diario!
Aunque a dos o tres le pese;
El cambio era necesario,
Por mas que algún adversario
Nos diga que no parece...
Si lo dice, es un cobarde
Falto de honor y vergüenza;
Pues es, sin hacer alarde,
¡diario único de la tarde!,
Desde este día, *La Prensa*.
Único en su información
De efectivo oportunismo,
Original redacción,
Y porque cada sección
Respira mexicanismo.

Porque la infamia rechaza
Y lleva siempre triunfante
El santo ideal que abraza:
¡POR LA PATRIA Y POR LA RAZA!
Y como lema: ¡ADELANTE!
      Llévese esta reprimenda
El malandrín atrevido
Que de algún modo pretenda
Tildarnos, para que entienda,
¡que no ha de buscarnos ruido!
      En esta misma sección
Y en verso no menos malo,
Voy a darle a la afición
Si me presta su atención,
Todos los días ¡un palo...!
      Y desde ahora le pido
A mis amables lectores
El más absoluto olvido
Si alguno resulta herido
Con estos palos "traidores"
Y les formulo este ruego
Por mis pupilas si brillo:
No giman, pues, si les pego,
Perdonen a un pobre ciego
Que no tiene lazarillo.

Junio 18 de 1922
Los Ángeles, Calif.

¡Ah qué don Félix!

Dicen los periódicos
Que don Félix Díaz
El presidenciable
De todos los días,
A México ha entrado
Con la pretensión
De encender de nuevo
La revolución (?),
Y por ese medio
Común y corriente
Realizar sus sueños
De ser Presidente.
¿Qué el pobre don Félix
Está muy choteado
Porque en sus delirios
Siempre ha fracasado?
¿Qué la Casa Blanca
Le dijo que "nones"
Porque ya no quiere
Más revoluciones?
Eso no le arredra
Y sigue en sus trece,
Y en vez de achicarse
El "héroe" se crece;
Y cuando desmaya,
Su ardor se revela
Al "santo" recuerdo
De la Ciudadela...
Y sigue de frente
Con la pretensión
De encender de nuevo
La revolución (?);
Para lo que cuenta
Con Pablo González,
Con Pancho Murguía

Y otros generales
De los que radican
En tierra extranjera
Mirando los toros
Desde la barrera,
Porque se imaginan
Que don Félix ya
Por donde se fue
Pronto volverá
A ensayar de nuevo
La vieja canción
De llevar a México
La revolución (?)...
Y por ese medio
Común y corriente
Realizar sus sueños
De ser Presidente
Déjele, don Félix,
Conquistar "la banda"
A su compañero
Zúñiga y Miranda.
Mientras tanto, búsquese
En el extranjero
Un medio decente
De ganar dinero,
Y si el infortunio
Su sueño desvela,
Invoque el recuerdo
De la Ciudadela...
Pero ya no siga
Con su pretensión
De encender de nuevo
La revolución (?)...

Junio 21 de 1922
Los Ángeles, Calif.

Trapitos al sol

Dice un refrán que el buen juez
Siempre empieza por su casa,
Y otro, que no hay peor astilla
Que la de la propia estaca;
Y como son los refranes
Breves y oportunas máximas
Sacadas de la experiencia,
(que lo diga Sancho Panza...),
Quiero, lector, aplicar,
Los dos refranes de marras,
Dedicando algunos "palos"
A las gentes de mi Raza
Que apenas llegan de México
Al país de Yanquilandia,
Olvidan el español
Y reniegan de su Patria;
Pero muy especialmente
Me referiré a la plaga
Que sin ningunos escrúpulos
Explota a la "paisanada"
Y como son tan variados
Los tipos de esa calaña,
Para no cansar al público
Voy a exhibirlos por tandas
A mis lindas paisanitas
Que usan muy corta la falda,
Y bailan el "Hula-Hula"
Y se embadurnan la cara,
Y se largan con el novio
Y se bañan en la playa,
Y mascan chicle, y se expresan
Con el idioma de Byron
Porque no saben "spanish",
Lo repito, a mis paisanas,
En atención a su sexo

No quiero decirles nada;
Y porque sé que con eso
Y todo, son mexicanas.
Tampoco quiero aludir
A las muy nobles ancianas
Que dicen que para México
(¡ay Dios!) "Ni volver la cara
Mientras las cosas no cambien";
Agregan las "diplomáticas"...
Y aludir no quiero a ellas
Pues... por respeto a sus canas.
Quede en paz el bello sexo;
Pero enderezo mi lanza
Contra aquellos renegados
Que se dicen de la raza
De Juárez y de Bolívar
Tan solo cuando se trata
De sacar algún provecho.
Por ejemplo: la "puntada"
De la corrida de toros
Que nos resultó una estafa;
Los famosos sanadores
Que curan hasta las ganas
Por medio de ciertos métodos...
Para sacar la "fierrada";
Ciertas logias mutualistas,
(no la Hispano-Americana
Ni otras más, muy honorables),
Que explotan a nuestra raza
A cambio de ofrecimientos,
Ilusiones y esperanzas,
Los judíos timadores
Revendedores de alhajas;
Ciertas agencias de empleos
Que al que se deja, lo enganchan:
Le ofrecen diez diarios,
Leña, luz, comida y casa,

Y dicen que está el trabajo
A diez millas de distancia,
Para salirle después
Con que van a Calipatria,
A pizcar melón, al raso
Del sol y casi por nada.
Contra todas esas gentes,
(perdonando la palabra...)
Y otras muchas que me callo,
Enderezaré mi lanza
En defensa de los nuestros,
POR LA PATRIA Y POR LA RAZA.
Y pongo punto final.
Hasta la siguiente tanda.

Los paisanos en las playas

1. Preparativos

— Anda, Timotea,
Hazme bien la raya
Para luego, luego
Irnos a la playa
Dame mi camisa
Color aceituna,
Y mis calcetines
Morados. Dale una
Planchada de paso
A mi pantalón.
¡Oye! mi mascada…
— ¡Hombre más molón!…

2. En el eléctrico

— Sube Timotea
Que se va el tranvía,
Agárrate juerte.
¡Anda Chemalía!
Que nos deja el tren.
¡Jesús que apretura!
No cabemos bien.
Ay! ay! ay! ¡Qué bruto!
Me reventó un callo
Ese mastodonte,
¡que lo parta un rayo!

3. En el balneario

— Válgame la virgen
Santísima, mira
Cómo andan "jirutos",
¡parece mentira!
Con razón les dicen
"bichis" a las playas,
Si andan todos "bichis"...
— ¡A ver si te callas!
Aquí, Timotea,
Todo es natural,
Todo se ve bien...
Nada se ve mal.
— Qué veo ¡Dios mío!
Mira a doña Chona,
Con ropa de baño
Y tan barrigona...
Anda, Chemalía
Vámonos de aquí,
Si no, el "accidente"
Me va a dar a mí.
— Ah! qué Timotea
Tan escrupulosa,
Tú te escandalizas
Por cualquier cosa.
— Pos a mí no "mentra"
La moda. ¿Qué queres?
Juera pa los hombres
No pa las mujeres!...
¿qué no te parece
A ti. Chemalía?
— No, porque la moda...
Pos... ¡se acabaría!...

4. En las rifas

Újule! Qué mala
Suerte tengo yo,
Se me jue un mugroso
De a diez; pero no
Le atiné al Cupido.
— Ni le atinarás,
Éstos lo que agarran
No güelve jamás.

5. En el salón de baile

— Válgame qué música
Toca en el salón,
Es mejor la orquesta
Del ciego Simón.
Mira cómo "la pata,
Diatiro parecen
Monos de hojalata.
— Antes ora, vieja,
Son más moderados,
Pos antiguamente
Bailaban pegados.

6. En la montaña rusa

— ¡Virgen del Socorro!
— Yo de ti me agarro;
Ora sí, viejito,
Nos mata este carro.
¡Ay Dios qué subidas!
¡ay Dios qué bajadas!
— Yo siento las tripas
Aquí en las quijadas.
— Oiga Míster, párele...
Se... se... se... señor...
Por San... Avagán
Hágame el favor.
Agárrame, Chémali,
Ya baja otra vez...
— ¡Újule!, parece
Qué me doy "las tres".
— Por fin el maldito
Carro se paró.
— ¿No das otra vuelta
Timotea?
— ¿Yo?
¡Primero difunta
Que volver aquí!
— Bueno, pos ya sabes,
No queda por mí...

Un sermón

Muy amadas hijas mías
Y hermanas en Jesucristo:
Nuestra Madre Iglesia manda
Que nosotros sus Ministros
Conduzcamos a los fieles
Siempre por el buen camino;
Que apartemos de su paso
Obstáculos y peligros
Que siembran las tentaciones
Sobre los flacos espíritus,
Que velemos por el prójimo
Como por nosotros mismos,
Y en fin, que seamos fieles
Representantes de Cristo.
Por eso quiero, hijas mías,
(después hablaré a mis hijos),
Daros algunos consejos
Que os salven del Enemigo
Asechador de virtudes
Y protector de los vicios.
Muy amadas hijas mías:
Con todo amor os conmino,
A que alarguéis vuestra falda
Siquiera algunos centímetros;
Pues veo por esas calles
De Dios, hermosos palmitos
De diez y seis a veinte años
Y hasta de cuarenta y pico,
(perdón por la irreverencia).
Que a juzgar por su vestido
Rabón, aún piden bombones
Y juegan al borriquito.

Que no pintéis vuestro rostro
Con esos tintes vivísimos

Que afean vuestros encantos
O maltratan vuestro físico;
Que no asistáis a los bailes
Con escotes tan... ridículos
Que exhiben lo que debiera
Permanecer nunca visto;
Que no bailéis ciertas piezas
Cuyos sones sicalípticos
Encienden las tentaciones
En los danzantes novicios;
Que a distancia moderada
Bailen (el baile a mi juicio
Es suave entretenimiento
Y saludable ejercicio
Que da vigor a los miembros
Y esparcimiento al espíritu,
Siempre que no rebasen
Las fronteras de lo lícito);
Pues sé que ciertas parejas
A pesar de lo prescrito
Por el último decreto
Dictado en ese sentido,
Bailan hasta el "Hula-Hula"
Sin dárseles un comino
Las censuras que provocan
En las gentes de buen juicio.
Dejo para otros sermón
Amadas hijas, deciros
Algo sobre la costumbre
De bañaros en los sitios
Públicos, donde naufraga
El pudor y triunfa el vicio.
Sea en el nombre del Padre,
Y también en el del Hijo
Y el del Espíritu Santo
Amén. Aquí me santiguo,
Con toda veneración,

Y "hasta verte Cristo mío."
Os manda su bendición
Vuestro padre:

FRAY-TORIBIO

Mejor chinos

Después de una pausa larga
De tres días,
Vuelvo, lector, a la carga
En esta labor amarga
De escribir "majaderías"
Contra aquellos de los nuestros
Que inhumanos,
Reniegan de sus ancestros
Y se erigen en maestros
Como malos mexicanos.

Hoy toca su turno a los
"Reaccionarios"
Que en "Don Félix" ven un dios.
Para muestra, allá van dos
De los más estrafalarios.

— "Las cosas van a cambiar
De seguro;
Ya don Félix ha de estar
En México, y debe obrar...
Porque es el caso de apuro...
Cuenta con mil Generales
Prestigiados (?)
De los viejos federales,
Con quinientos oficiales
Y ciento veinte soldados.

Y con semejante tropa
El "Caudillo"
Podrá conquistar Europa,
Como quien toma una copa
De excelente "curadillo"...

— Lo malo es que le faltó…
El apoyo
De Washington, ¡que sé yo!
— ¡Cierto! Por más que ofreció
Lo mandaron al arroyo.

Sin embargo, si esta vez
No hay victoria,
Ya triunfaremos después;
Que dos lustros, cinco, diez,
No son nada ante la Historia…

Contra la revolución
Marcharemos;
Y venga la Intervención.
Hay que tocar los extremos
Si al fin triunfa la Reacción.

Y si no llega ese día
Yo prefiero
Perder mi ciudadanía.
— Yo también preferiría
Antes hacerme extranjero.

(Los dos a coro);
Con Don Félix, mexicanos,
Y sin él,
Chinos, norte-americanos,
Ingleses… hasta paisanos
Del mismísimo Luzbel.

"Las cosas van a cambiar
De seguro
Pues don Félix ha de estar
En México, y debe obrar…
Porque es el caso de apuro…"

José Fonseca

Lector amable:
Abro un paréntesis
En estos "palos",
Para ofrecerle
Un justo elogio
Al más valiente,
Al más intrépido
De nuestros héroes
De la quinta arma:
Esto refiérese
Al mexicano
Aviador célebre,
(solo al decirlo
Gusto se siente),
José Fonseca,
Quien hizo en "Vénis"
Vuelos audaces
Y sorprendentes.
Miradlo: sube
Sereno y fuerte,
Sonríe al público,
Luego se mece
Sobre los aires;
Vienen las suertes
Escalofriantes
Que entre las gentes
Siembran el pánico.
Ved: de repente
Da el "loop de loop",
Y se suspende
Por los talones
Sin que le arredre
No tener nada
Que lo sujete;
Y así ejecuta

Todas sus suertes,
Frío e impasible
Ante la muerte,

Veinte mil almas
Han ido a Vénis
Por ver proezas
De nuestro héroe,
Quien para el próximo
Domingo ofrece
Nuevas sorpresas
De las que tiene
Él para ciertos
Casos solemnes...

¡Gloria al paisano!
¡Honor al héroe!
Que honor y gloria
Justa merecen,
Los compatriotas
Que como éste
Honran a México
En lo que pueden...
Donde tan poco
Se nos comprende...
Y decir saben
Cómo se aprende
A sonreírse
Ante la muerte!...

El radio

"Palabras que de allá vienen
Palabras que de aquí van,
Si en el camino se encuentran
¿cuántas veces chocarán...?

Todo el mundo está "lelo"
Con el nuevo aparato
Que trasmite las ondas
Hertzianas: el Radio;
Las cuales se reciben
Desde puntos lejanos
Maravillosamente;
Pues la música, el canto
Y cualquier otro ruido
Se perciben tan claros
Y distintos, que cuando
Llegan a nuestro oído
Nos parece que estamos
Bajo el dulce conjuro
De algún sueño fantástico.

Ayer precisamente
Pude oír el milagro
En el laboratorio
De un amable paisano
Y amigo, que invitóme
Para mostrarme el Radio,
Y en verdad os lo digo:
Quedé maravillado.
Repito, es asombroso
Ese nuevo aparato;
Mas como todo tiene
Siempre su lado malo,
Con ser un gran prodigio,

También lo tiene el Radio
Para probarlo a ustedes
Aquí cito dos casos.

La señora de X
Pretende oír un rato
La audición del Examiner,
Pero ¡ay! al intentarlo
Percibe claramente
La voz de don Mariano
Su esposo, que platica
Junto a algún aparato
Transmisor.
Anda — dice, —
"el muy desvergonzado,"
Vámonos a Venecia,
Ya son las seis y cuarto;
Allá cenamos juntos
Y después regresamos
De pasar un buen tiempo;
Y contesta en el acto
Una voz femenina:
— Pero si usté es casado…
Y si su esposa sabe
Estas cosas… ¡Dios Santo!
¿qué va a decir? — ¿Mi esposa?
¡que se la lleve el diablo!

Días después la cara
Mitad de don Mariano
Pide el divorcio. Todo
Por el maldito Radio…

— Mujer, ya son las ocho
Y mira, no he cenado,
Llegué desde las cinco
Rendido de cansancio,

Y en vez de prepararme
La cena, ¡voto al chápiro!
Estás oyendo pláticas
Y músicas y cantos.
— ¡Silencio! No hagas ruido
Que está cantando Lázaro...
Te vas a la cocina
Con cien mil de a caballo
O desde ahora mismo
Te casas con el Radio!...

Por sabido se calla
Lector, que en estos casos
No quedan comprendidos
Nuestros primos...hermanos.

Agoreros de males

Cuando el señor De la Huerta
Salió para Nueva York
A arreglar con los banqueros
Lo de la deuda exterior,
Los enemigos de México,
Los tigres de la Reacción,
Rieron desdeñosamente
Y levantaron su voz
Augurándole un fracaso
A nuestro Ministro, por
No tener los altos vuelos
(ni las agallas "ad hoc")
De aquel genio en las finanzas
Que se llamó "Limantour",
Genio que don Luis Cabrera
Supo aprovechar mejor...
Y gritaban obcecados:
— ¿De la Huerta a Nueva York
A tratar con los más grandes
Financieros? ¡Uf! ¡Qué horror!
¡Qué sorpresas nos prepara
El Gobierno de Obregón!
Y seguían desbarrando
Así por ese tenor
Los enemigos de México,
Los lobos de la Reacción.

Hoy que el señor De la Huerta,
Sin las agallas "ad hoc",
Sin la ciencia financiera
Ni el genio de "Limantour"
Puso a flote nuestra deuda
Dando prestigio y honor
A nuestra Patria, los mismos
Chacales de la Reacción,

Cegados por el despecho
Pretenden tapar el sol
Con un dedo, asegurando
Que México fracasó,
Y que si acaso hubo arreglo
Debe ser a condición
De un "sacrificio muy grande"
Por parte de la Nación...
Sigan ladrando a la luna
Los canes de la Reacción,
Soñando con el milagro
De una existencia mejor...

La ola del crimen

En la ciudad divina
De los balnearios
Y los parques exhúberos
De hermosos lagos,
En la bella angelópolis
Que bajo el manto
De las nieblas se cubre
Como en su blanco
Traje una desposada,
Se ha desbordado
La ola roja del crimen,
Y está sembrando
Entre las gentes buenas
Terror y espanto.
Hoy, dos o tres apaches
Roban un banco
En pleno día, luego
Son dos muchachos
Que asaltan el correo
O el "Wells & Fargo";
Ora es una señora
Que a la de al lado,
Sin mediar una frase,
Le da un balazo
Porque — según declara —
Se lo ha mandado
El espíritu X
O el mismo diablo.
Ora los "Barba-Azules"
Surgen flotando
En un río de sangre,
Y mientras tanto,
Una dama "sin barba"
Ha confesado
Que se casó diez veces,

Que sus incautos
Ex-maridos murieron
Achicharrados
En el horno que tiene
Para estos casos.

Pero ningún suceso
De los citados,
Ha tenido la fuerza
Del registrado
Hace apenas tres días.
Todos los diarios,
"La Prensa" antes que todos
Ya publicaron
El crimen espantoso:
El soplo trágico
De los celos apaga
"Los fuegos fatuos
De la razón." Un brazo
Que se alza amenazante;
Ved: en la mano
Blanca y ebúrnea lleva
La muerte. Abajo
Una mujer que implora
Piedad, en vano;
De repente, violento
Como el relámpago
Sobre la desgraciada
Cae aquel brazo
Y la asesta un terrible
Golpe en el cráneo:
Flor sangrienta que se abre
Bajo el espasmo
Del crimen. Y otro golpe,
Luego otros varios,
Hasta que sólo quedan
Sucios guiñapos

Llenos de sangre y lodo
Y salpicados
Por la masa encefálica.
¡Horrible cuadro!
Una dama que a otra
Pide su auto
Para dar un paseo,
Premeditando
Asesinarla, sólo
Porque ha pensado
Que enamora a su esposo.

Y consumando
Su intento, la asesina
¡a martillazos!!

La suegra de Bruno

Mi amigo Bruno Valente
Me escribe de Santa Paula,
Quejándose amargamente
De su suegra, pues se siente
Como pájaro en la jaula
Desde que su suerte negra
O el mismísimo demonio
Que todo lo desintegra,
— me dice — mezcló a su suegra
En su feliz matrimonio.

Pero dejemos a Bruno
La palabra hasta el final;
Y ya verán que el muy tuno
Se queja como ninguno
De la vida conyugal.

"Mañana hará un año justo
Que me casé con Teodora,
Una chica encantadora
Que tuvo el pésimo gusto
De llamarse mi señora.

Y vaya que nos queremos,
Tanto, que no hay más que ver,
Pues en soltando los remos
Del cariño, ni comemos
Por darle vuelo al querer.

— ¡Eres mi único embeleso!
— ¡mi "kuppie"!
— ¡Pichona mía!
— Dame un beso...otro...

— ¡Otro beso!
Y en este dulce "intermezzo"
Pasábamos todo el día.

Mas como nunca se alcanza
Completa felicidad,
De pronto, nuestra esperanza
Se hunde al ver en lontananza
Barruntos de tempestad;

Pues quiso mi suerte negra
O el mismísimo demonio
Que todo lo desintegra,
Introducir a mi suegra
En mi feliz matrimonio.

Ella ordena, pone y quita
A su entera voluntad
Y a todo el mundo le grita.
¡Qué mujer! ¡Virgen Bendita!
Es una calamidad.

¡Oh! mi suegra en su furor
Bate el "record" de las suegras
Y gana el premio mayor.
Yo lo tengo más horror
Que a un toro de Piedras Negras.

Desde que la condenada
Se ha erigido en juez y jefe
De mi tétrica morada,
Soy un pobre mequetrefe
Que no sirvo para nada.

Se enfurece si hablo poco,
Si hablo mucho, me alza el grito,
Si canto, que soy un loco,

Si fumo, náuseas provoco
Y en fin, ¡que me tiene frito!

Si salgo, tuerce la jeta,
Si no salgo, se encopeta
Por si sigue la retreta
Fusilar a esta señora.

Sí, la mato en cualquier rato:
La ahorco o le doy cianuro
O a martillazos la mato:
(El sistema más barato
Para salir del apuro).

Después se sabrá que un yerno
Que sufrió la pena negra,
Se ha librado del Infierno
Asesinando a su suegra
Por el sistema moderno."

Y el pobre Bruno bosqueja
Al final de su misiva,
La siguiente moraleja,
En la cual nos aconseja
En forma muy expresiva:

"Si procuras compañera
Porque así a tu gusto cuadre
O porque el diablo lo quiera,
Apechuga con cualquiera
¡Pero que no tenga madre...!"

Las espiritistas de Bacerac

Toda la prensa
Dio la noticia,
De que en Sonora
Dos señoritas
Interesantes,
Guapas y lindas,
Por los espíritus
Son perseguidas.
Que a todas horas:
De noche y día
Las atormentan
Con peregrinas
Insinuaciones;
Y las pellizcan,
Y las detienen
Cuando caminan.
Si es en la mesa,
¡Virgen Bendita!
Sienten que cerca
Alguien respira,
Y cuando menos
Se lo imaginan.
Todos los trastos
De la cocina
Vuelan y chocan
Y se hacen trizas.
Si es en la cama,
Oyen terríficas
Imprecaciones,
Quejas que enchinan
La piel, y luego
Cantos y risas,
Y como que les
Hacen cosquillas.
Naturalmente

Las pobres víctimas
De los espíritus
Bolchevikistas,
Se están quedando
Como una espina;
Y hechas espíritus
Se quedarían
Si no cesaran
Sus tristes cuitas.
Pero por suerte
De las dos niñas
Un respetable
Capitalista
Que tiene rachas
De espiritista,
A la Metrópoli
Va a remitirlas,
Para que estudie
La medicina
El caso raro
Que se consigna

Lo más curioso
De la noticia,
Es que la abonan
Como verídica
Personas serias,
Quienes afirman
Que esto ha pasado
Ante su vista.
Así lo dicen
Los periodistas
Que nunca cuentan
Una mentira...

Aunque las gentes
Tomen a risa

Las mencionadas
Chocarrerías,
El caso es serio:
Dos señoritas
Interesantes,
Guapas y lindas
Que en esa forma
Son perseguidas,
Sin que se sepa
Quién las hostiga,
Debe atendérselas,
Pero en seguida.
¡Quién fuera médico
O espiritista!

Porque "semos" de allá...

— Señor Magistrado:
He pedido audiencia,
Con el fin de suplicarle
A su excelencia,
Se me dé el empleo
Que dejó vacante
Al ser ascendido
Manuel Escalante.
Infórmese usted
Por el nombramiento
Y las referencias
Que aquí le presento,
De mis aptitudes
Y de mi honradez.
El Jefe se entera
Y dice después:
— Es usted un joven
Muy aprovechado,
Pero antes que nada
Dígame su Estado.
— Señor, soy soltero.
— Su Estado natal.
— Yo soy de Jalisco.
— Pues... ahí está el mal.
— ¿Cuál es el motivo?
— No siga adelante;
Lo siento muchísimo
Pero no hay vacante.

Señor; aquí traigo
Este nombramiento
Para que lo firme
— Espere un momento.
Muy bien. Enterado.
¿Qué sabe usté hacer?

— Pues con su permiso
"escribir" y "leer."
También sé contar
Con tal "corrección"
Que puedo jugarle
A cualquier gallón.
— ¿Es usté taquígrafo?
¿Sabe redactar?
¿Escribe usté en máquina?
— Para comenzar
Sé lo suficiente.
— Dígame usté ahora:
¿ "actual" es su Estado?
¡Yo soy de Sonora!...
— Por ahí debía
Haber empezado
Desde este momento
Queda usted empleado.

Eche usted nombre de frutas

Pedro **Limón** fue a Tex-**coco**
Con su novia Rosa **Piña**,
(los nombres de frutas van
— favor —, con letra cursiva),
Una muchacha **man-zana**
Que una rosa de Castilla,
Y más **fresa** que la aurora;
Y allá hablaron de esta guisa;

— Díme con toda **frambuesa**
Pera dímelo en seguida:
¿es exacto que **uvalamas**
A esa mujer de Co-**lima**
Que se **guayaba** contigo
Muy **mamey** el otro día?
Melón contado todito;
ci-ruela la bola **a-sína** (1)
¿pa qué de-**moras** conmigo?
Anda y vete con la **I-sidra**
Y gasta tu **plata, — no?**
— ¡Ay **bachata** (2) de mi vida!
Con tus cuentos **chabacanos**
No se lo-**granada**; mira,
Pasa y siéntate a mi lado
Y **frambuesa**-me, Rosita.
— No me **papaches**, y vete
A que te bese la **I-sidra**.
— ¡**Dur-aznos** Dios 'conpartícipes'
De tu Reino. ¡Bachatita!
¡Déjate de **chirimoyas**!
Oyeme, no seas **sandía**-,
Ya le hablé a tu **papá-yo**,
Y, — **ceresa** nuestra dicha —
Me dijo luego: "**higo** mío,
Anda y cásate en se-**guinda**".

¿Qué es-**peras**, pues, que no sales?
Ven a la **jamaica**, chica,
A echar una **caña** al aire;
Bailemos un **mango**: ¿anímate!
Albérchigo-zamos, Rosa,
Donde la gente se a-**piña**;
Pues tú bien sabes cuán **brevas**
Son las **moras** de esta vida.

Nuez que te desprecie, Pedro,
Pera, ¿y si viene la **I-sidra**?
— Es **banana** tu aprehensión.
— Tú **avellanas** en seguida
Todo, y con tu **persimonia**
Me haces contestar que **sí-nas**.
— ¡Bien **pita-haya** tu querer!
¡**Tú-na** sabes mi alegría!
Amame-y...

— que no te jale
La **grosella** de la **I-sidra,**
Uva-**mos** a quebrar.
— Yo,
Seré siempre, **nuez** mentira.
Quien te **uva**-l-ama con toda
La **almendra** ba-**chata** mía!...

Junio de 1923

Míster BLIND

(1-2) Frutas silvestres de Sonora.

¿Secos o Mojados?

— En Yanquilandia
Todo está seco;
La "Ley Volstead"
Mandó al Infierno
Vino y borrachos
Desde hace tiempo:
Ley sapientísima
Digna de ejemplo.
Gracias a ella
No padecemos
Una cantina
Cada seis metros,
Por las calles
Andan haciendo
"equis" y "zetas"
Ebrias y ebrios.
Ya los domingos
No van a Vernon
Por Centenares
En los eléctricos
Las caravanas
Que en otros tiempos
Allá tenían
Su abrevadero...
En los balnearios
Tampoco vemos
Los cuadros "plásticos"
De antaño: cientos
De intoxicados
De los dos sexos
Que se exhibían
En el paseo.
Hoy todo el mundo
Se siente bueno
Fuera del radio

Del vicio horrendo...
Esto decía
Yo a Míster Benson,
Un mi vecino
Muy parrandero
Que siempre anda,
(¿se admite el término?),
"a medios chiles";
Y haciendo un gesto
Muy expresivo
Contesta luego:
— Oiga, vecino,
¿qué está diciendo?
¿Qué ya no hay vino?
¿Qué ya no hay ebrios?
Usté me quiere
Tomar el pelo.
Mire Usté: ahora
Que estamos secos
Hay más borrachos
Que en otros tiempos,
Sólo que ahora,
— del mal el menos —
Se bebe poco
Porque el "veneno"
Es más activo
Y es mas su precio
¿Qué no se miran
Ebrias ni ebrio
Por esas calles
Como antes? Cierto;
En cambio ahora
Es un expendio
De bebestibles
Con kick, del bueno,
Cada hotelucho,
Y hay mil quinientos

Donde se embriagan
"ellas" y "ellos";
Lo cual se llama
Barrer "pa dentro."
Por otra parte,
— siguió diciendo
Con agrio tono —;
Sin el impuesto
De los alcoholes
Pierde el Gobierno
Muchos millones,
Y, sin remedio,
Al nivelarse
Los presupuestos,
Suben los "taxes"
Al quinto cielo,
Y al fin el pato
Lo paga el pueblo.

Aquí dejamos
A Míster Benson
En punto y coma;
Pues, extranjeros
En Yanquilandia,
Sólo tenemos
Para sus leyes
Y reglamentos,
Buenos o malos,
Nuestro respeto.

Los Apochados

Hay en Estados Unidos
Mucho bueno que imitar,
Si hemos de hablar en justicia
Y en nombre de la verdad.
Para citar solo un caso,
Y de momento, ahí está
El hábito del trabajo
Y las ansias de guardar
El dólar, nikel a nikel
Con pasmosa habilidad,
En lo que piadosamente
Lo permite el capital;
Hábito que viene a ser
La mejor seguridad
Del futuro, siempre incierto
En todo medio social.

Algunos otros ejemplos
Aquí podría citar;
Pero con el anterior
Entiendo que bastará
Para que se vea que hablo
Con toda imparcialidad.

Quiero ahora referirme
A los que vienen "de allá"
Y en vez de imitar lo bueno
Que aquí observan, siempre van
Copiando lo peor. ¿Ejemplos?
No se necesitan hurgar
Mucho para descubrirlos,
Pues de que los hay los hay.

Pero antes de dar con ellos
Permíteme presentar

En escena un nuevo tipo
No menos original.

¿Ven ustedes aquel joven
Que masca... ¿qué mascará?
Debe ser tabaco o chicle
Que para el caso es igual;
Lo acompaña una damita
Falta de carnes y edad,
(hasta un ciego lo adivina),
Cuyo rostro angelical,
(es un decir), desparece
Bajo una capa de cal
Y colorete; la falda
Me permite adivinar
La posición de las ligas
Que se alejan más y más
Como "las aves marinas
(¡perdón!), con rumbo hacia allá"...
El escote exagerado,
Casi, casi al natural
Y... ¡caramba! Me olvidaba
Que he prometido callar
Las "flaquezas" de las damas;
Y las pido una vez más
Disimulen loe errores
De mi memoria fatal.

Usando de este perdón
Permítanme continuar.
Como no se ha satisfecho
Toda mi curiosidad
Por lo que mira a la tierna
Pareja citada ya,
Quiero oír lo que platican
Me acerco, y escucho:

— "All right"
"Me hablas por el **telefon**
Ai one seven O three nine
Y me dices si agarrastes
El **aromobil** del **Sam,**
Pa ponerme muy jaitona
Y que nos demos un **raid**
En los **biches...**
— **Sabes Marry?**
Y no te enojes **"sweet heart"**
Por lo que voy a **decirte:**
I dont Know si iremos.
— **What?**
Entonces eres muy cheap...
!Mira que **sanavagán!**
¿**Pareso** me **alborotates?**
¿**What su mara? ¡¡Chises cráis!!**

En ese momento pasa,
(maldita casualidad),
Un auto de la Cruz Roja
Y no me deja oír más.

Y como esto se prolonga
Pongo aquí punto final.

Películas cortas

Voy a copiar en seguida
Los cuadros del natural
Que dan colorido y vida
A la calle principal,
En el espacio que queda
Entre la "first" y la Plaza.
En la "New High" y "Alameda"
Y otras de importancia escasa,
En donde nuestros paisanos
Que no conocen el medio
Se entregan de pies y manos
A los "vivos", sin remedio.

— "Vestido entera diez pesos
Lo mismo que aparador.
Pónese el saco, señor:
Mira: la forro muy gruesos.
Muy bonita; sube más.

Frente muy bien; no mentira.
(Al decir esto le estira
Seis pulgadas por detrás).
Ahora mira el espejo,
"Espalda muy elegante."
(Aquí le recoge el viejo
Seis pulgadas por delante).
Y si no hay quien ilumine
Al paisano, se va al viaje;
Es decir, se compra un traje
Para el Gordito del cine.

— Este reloj puro plata,
Cien años por garantía.
(Y al cliente le dura un día).

— Pasen a oír la pianola.
No necesitan dinero.
(Entran y se hace la bola
Y dejan hasta el sombrero).

— Cuatro reales por cabeza.
— Ya se completó la pinta.
— Ya me lleva la tristeza
De puro crudo.

Otra cinta

— ¡A la pizca de algodón!
¡Cinco pesos el quintal!...
(Y van al Valle Imperial
Y ahí se hacen la ilusión...)

Me seduce tu mirada
Chaparrita encantadora.
(Toman una limonada
Y platican media hora.)

— ¿Oyes el Himno, aparcero?
— Aquí sacando retrato,
Muy bonita, muy barato.
(Y les sacan su dinero.)

Dejo en cartera otros tipos
De confección especial
Porque ya los linotipos
Me piden original.

¿A mí qué?...

¿Que los ferrocarrileros
Nacionales y extranjeros
Se declararon en huelga,
Y que el Gobierno los cuelga
Por causas que yo no sé?
¿A mí qué?

¿Qué las testigos de cargo
Le brinden un rato amargo
A la "Dama del Martillo"
Que a l'otra hizo picadillo,
Porque del crimen dan fe?
¿A mí qué?

¿Qué en los balnearios exhiben,
Porque no se los prohiben,
Sus encantos las bañistas?
¿Qué por eso los "touristas"
Ahí van, por lo que se ve?
¿A mí qué?

¿Que temiendo un "mal encuentro"
Ha desertado del "Centro
Hispano y Americano"
Cierto grupo mexicano
Que nos quiere dar café?
¿A mí qué?

¿Que algunos de mis paisanos
Que parecen cuadrumanos
Y comen puros frijoles
Digan que son españoles
Y contesten "Juat chu sey"?
¿A mí qué?

¿Que en la calle de "New High"
Le dicen a usted "good by"
Y lo jalan de la cola
Y le tocan la pianola
Y no sale por su pie?
¿A mí qué?

¿Que con sus cortos vestidos
Parecen "Kuppies" (Cupidos),
Y abusan del bermellón
De los polvos y el crayón
Ciertas damas que yo sé?
¿A mí qué?

¿Que en la tienda de ocasión
Compra usted un pantalón,
Y al estrenarlo, ve al punto
Que era más grande el difunto,
Y grita y reniega usté?
A mí qué?

¿Qué dos o tres vividores
Como en "épocas mejores"
"por patriotismo" hacen "algo"
Para festejar a Hidalgo,
Y hay quien dinero les dé?
¿A mí qué?

¿En fin, que este "ritornelo"
Les pone de punta el pelo
A tres o cuatro "endevidos"
Que se sienten aludidos
Y se me vienen de frente?
Eso sí, ya es diferente...

Porque no hay campanas...

Todos conocen
El cuento aquel
Del sacerdote
Que fue una vez
A cierto pueblo
Y vio que en él
No repicaban;
Buscó el por qué
De aquella falta,
Y un feligrés
Así le dijo
Con mucha fe:
— Pues las razones,
Padre, son tres:
QUE NO HAY CAMPANAS
Primero.
— Pues
Con eso basta
Para saber
Cuál de la falta
La causa es.

Un comerciante
De esta Babel
Me dijo un día:
— No sé qué hacer:
Bajan las ventas
Y cada vez
Suben los "taxes"
Más, y también
Las rentas suben
Y suben. Es
Casi imposible

Nuestro sostén.
¿Cómo pudiera
Yo resolver
Este problema,
Dígame usted?
Y parodiando
Al feligrés
De las campanas
Le dije: pues
Por tres razones
No vende usted:
Porque no anuncia,
Una. Porque
No anuncia, dos,
Y por fin, tres,
Porque no anuncia
Ya tiene usted
Las tres razones
De que le hablé.

Y si el anuncio
La clave es
De los negocios
En cualesquier
Forma, es seguro
Que en el "papel"
(como aquí dicen),
Produce cien
Veces su costo
Y más tal vez

Y si en *La Prensa*
Se anuncia usted,
(Aquí anunciamos
Barato y bien),

Se hace usted rico
En dos por tres. *

Julio 27 de 1922
Los Angeles, Calif.

Míster BLIND
(Agente General de Anuncios)

* *Esto quiere decir que se anuncie usted cuando menos en un espacio de dos pulgadas por tres columnas...más o menos, a elección.*

Los caseros

Ya piden misericordia
Los vecinos de este pueblo,
Por el abuso inaudito
De los señores caseros,
Que sin temor a las llamas
Vengadoras del infierno,
Suben y suben las rentas
Hasta los séptimos cielos.
¡Y qué casas! Hay jonucos
Que rentan cincuenta pesos
Con tres piezas solamente,
¡Y qué piezas! ¡Padre Eterno!
Una salita rabona,
El piso pegado al techo,
Recámara al aire libre
(muy higiénica por cierto);
La cocina es un huacal
Por donde entra y sale el viento
Como Pedro por su casa;
El "reservado" a dos metros
Del comedor. A estos agréguese
El constante taconeo
De los vecinos de arriba;
Pues la casa que bosquejo
Es de dos pisos. El "toilet"
Es de sistema moderno,
Ya que al funcionar nos brinda
Un baño de cuerpo entero;
Además, hay la ventaja
De despertar siempre a tiempo
Si se quiere madrugar,
Sin el timbre, tan molesto,
Que el repicar de la chinches
Lo tendrán a usted despierto.

Y no se le ocurra a usted
Llevar chamacos pequeños,
(puede usted criar sin peligro,
Pericos, gatos y perros);
Los cuales gozan aquí
De inalienables derechos;
Pero llevar a la casa
A sus niños ¡vade retro!
Ni pensarlo, porque entonces
Llega furioso el casero,
Le dice que a los vecinos
Se les malorea el sueño,
Que los chamacos despintan
Pisos, paredes y techo...
Y en fin, que deje la casa
Antes del día primero
O l'echa los muebles fuera,
Y ya está usted en aprietos,
¡todo por tener chamacos
Que no crecieron a tiempo...!

Lástima que aquí no haya
Sindicatos como aquellos
De resultados tan prácticos,
Que se organizan en México...

De México a Los Ángeles, Calif.

"Compadre Tobías;
Le pongo esta carta
Para noticiarle
Que estamos en Jauja,
Desde que nos dieron
Tierras, paz y agua:
La verdad le digo:
Aquí no se ganan
Dólares, ni tienen
Como allá las casas
"porche", y sacatito
Y otras zarandajas,
Edificios de esos
Tan altos, que espantan,
Y nos destantean,
No hay en nuestra patria;
Pero aquí circula
Peritita plata
Y hermosos "Aztecas";
En cuanto a las casas,
Hay en las "Colonias"
"chaletes" que encantan
Y que son por dentro
Unas filigranas.
¿Y nuestros palacios?
Viendo sus fachadas
A los extranjeros
Se les cae la baba...
Aquí no tenemos,
(¡Qué suerte tan mala!),
Ni los bellos parques
Ni las lindas playas
En donde se exhiben
Las carnes más blancas...;
En cambio gozamos

De los panoramas
Divinos, espléndidos
De nuestras montañas;
Y hay un Xochimilco,
(figúrese, ¡nada!),
Y un "Bosque", testigos
De glorias pasadas,
Que no los cambiamos,
(por mi madre santa);
Ni por Míster Wilson;
Y tantas, y tantas
Cosas que tenemos
Nosotros guardadas
En esta bendita
Tierra del Anáhuac.
Véngase, compadre,
Aunque ya no traigan
De balde como antes,
Junte la "fierrada"
Y si no se ajusta
Póngase una carta
Para remitirle
Lo que le haga falta.
Contésteme luego.
Dígame qué pasa
Con los cien dólares
Que mandé a mi casa
Cuando estaba en esa.
La Prensa nos daba
La nueva que el banco
Que el di las platas
Quebró, y nos dejaron
A los de la Raza,
Como los caimanes.
Abriendo las tapas...
Y hasta la siguiente.

Con gusto lo abraza
Su compadre Pedro
Rodríguez Aranda "

De Los Ángeles a México

Querido compadre:
Recibí con retraso su carta,
En la cual me platica de cosas
Que llegan al alma:
De mi Xochimilco
Donde tengo mis cuatro chinampas
Y una anciana que espera mi vuelta:
¡Mi madre adorada!
Me habla usted del Bosque,
De los lagos y de las montañas
Y del cielo divino de México,
Y mire: las lágrimas.
Oyendo esas cosas,
Se me salen del fondo del alma.
Le agradezco lo de los pasajes.
De veras es lástima
Que no puedan darnos
El pasaje como antes nos daba,
Nada más porque algunos paisanos
Meten la cizaña
Y a "lora de lora"
Cuando llegan los barcos, nos ganan,
Y se van para México, y vuelven
A las dos semanas;
Pues van a pasearse
Y entre tanto nosotros, ya liadas
Las maletas, aquí nos quedamos
Abriendo las tapas...
Qué bueno sería
Que el Gobierno otra vez decretara
Repatriarnos, poniendo el asunto
En manos honradas...

Respecto a su encargo
Del girito que dices, no hay nada;

Pues el banco quebró, como sabe
Y se hundió la barca.
Varios abogados
Están viendo, compadre, si salvan
Una parte siquiera del buque,
Pero... ¡ni esperanzas!
Síganme escribiendo;
No se enfade, compadre. Sus cartas
Mensajeras de amor y alegría
Son en esta casa;
Porque en ellas vienen
El olor de mis verdes chinampas,
De mi madre el recuerdo, y la Gloria
Que envuelve a mi Raza.

Sígame escribiendo
De esas cosas que llegan al alma,
Y reciba un abrazo afectuoso
Su compadre:

Matías Lizárraga

SEGUNDO PARTE

SECOND PART.

El sofocante calor de Mexicali

El sofocante calor
Del ígneo Valle Imperial,
Es un calor infernal
Que hace cambiar de color
Al más "pintado" mortal.

El sol del África, cuna
Del negro de "Flor de un Día",
Aquel sol, no es sol, es luna
Si se compara con una
Asoleada a medio día
En este bendito Valle
De lamentos y...sudores.

¿Qué más? Va usted por la calle
Y no da un paso sin que halle
Tres o cuatro valedores,
Con ambas cuencas vacías
Y más tiesos que una reata:
Si el diablo en sus correrías
Vive aquí dos o tres días
También estira la pata.
Y no es exageración,
Digo la verdad desnuda,
En esta ardiente región,
Se "pela", aquel que no suda,
Por "evaporación".

Si busca usted un consuelo
En el baño, es inconcuso
Que si no le pone hielo,
Se da usted un baño ruso
Y deja en el baño el pelo.

Huyendo de los calores
Que tanto el sistema excitan,
Para hablar de sus amores
Los pobres novios se citan
En los refrigeradores,
Por que ya cierta pareja
Al darse un ardiente beso,
Quedó tan solo por eso,
Untada sobre la reja
De donde pasó el suceso.

Esta calor endiablada
Nos pone fuera de sí;
Vean ustedes: (no es tanteada);
¡todo el mundo huele aquí
A bistec y carne asada!...
Si en un refrigerador
Guarda usted blanquillos nuevos,
(¡poderosa incubadora!)
En menos de media hora
Empollan todos los huevos...!

En las horas del calor
Que son todas las de día
Y de la noche, que es peor,
Se observan casos, lector,
De rara psicología.

Un ejemplo: los pedantes,
Los banqueros orgullosos
Que no saludaban antes,
Con el calor son galantes,
Corteses y hasta obsequiosos,
Esto en el tercer período
De insolación se comprende:
Cuando el espíritu todo

Se desintegra, de modo
Que en dulce igualdad se enciende.

Otro ejemplo: los políticos
Proveedores del Congreso,
El domingo, en casos críticos;
"gordos," "flacos" y "raquíticos,"
Casi se daban un beso...

Ahora diga el lector
Si el sofocante calor
Del ígneo Valle Imperial,
No hará "cambiar de color"
Al más "pintado" mortal.

El incendio de "El Tecolote"

"En noche de densa bruma
Un "tecolote" se ardió,
Y el cuerpo se consumió
Sin quemarse ni una pluma"...

Después del incendio
De hace algunos días,
En que varias casas
Quedaron en ruinas,
(que lo digan Monjo,
El doctor Molina,
Los del Monte-Carlo
Y los de en seguida,
Y si no lo dicen...
Pues... que no lo digan)
Un nuevo siniestro
Redujo a cenizas
Toda la manzana
En donde tenían
Su asiento los juegos,
Donde todavía
Las "mujeres malas"
Estaban recluidas.
El hotel de Arturo
Him Sam Lung fue víctima
También del incendio;
Pero a grande prisa
Fue aislado. Acudieron
Como las avispas
Mil quinientos chinos
Armados de picas,
Baldes y sartenes,
Logrando en seguida
Sofocar el fuego,
Que si no se aísla

Acaba con todos
Los hijos de China...
Comenzó el incendio,
(y el caso se explica),
Por la sofocantes
Casas de las pípilas.
Funcionaron todas
Las bombas que había,
Pero no lograron
Llenar la medida,
Ni las bombas grandes
Ni las bombas chicas;
Fueron impotentes
Tanto las vecinas
Como las locales,
Ya ni las cenizas
Quedan de la crótica
"ave de rapiña."
Se estiman las pérdidas.

El domingo azul

Los moralistas
De Yanquilandia
Han emprendido
Dura campaña
Contra los vicios
Feos que matan
A los mortales
En cuerpo y alma.
Y al fin tan noble
Va encaminada
La ley que ordena
Que de su casa
Nadie en domingo
Un paso salga,
Si no es al templo
A elevar santas
Preces al cielo,
Dulces plegarias
Porque se limpien
Como con agua
Y "lye", (lejía),
Todas las almas.

Nadie irá al cine
Ni irá a las playas
Ni irá a los parques
Sin grave falta;
Porque en los cines
El diablo anda
Metiendo el rabo
Y hurtando almas;
Porque el pecado
Vive en las playas
Y en los "cafeses"
Donde se baila

El "shimie" y otras
Lúbricas danzas;
Que a los parques
Van las muchachas
Y el aire puro
Las entusiasma,
Y sienten dulces,
Íntimas ansias;
Y ahí los viejos
Y las ancianas
Hacen recuerdos
De las pasadas
Horas felices
De paz y calma.

Todo sujeto
Que sus miradas
Fije en las ligas
De ciertas damas,
(sigue diciendo
La ley de marras),
Será multado
En veinte "piastras".
Veinte dólares
Es la palabra;
Pero usar quise
La mencionada
Por exigencias
De la asonancia.
Esta "figura"
Ripio se llama.)
A tal extremo
Dicen que alcanzan
Los rigorismos
De la campaña,
Que en el "Blue Sunday",
— como se llaman

Al santo día
En Yanquilandia —
Ni los canarios
Ni las canarias
Habitar deben
La misma jaula;
Pues si se besan,
Las iras santas
Harán su agosto
Sobre sus almas.

¡Pobres Canarios...!
Ni aun en la jaula
La ley los deja
Vivir en calma...

Crónicas de "Base Ball"

La segunda Serie de la Liga
Del Valle Imperial,
Dígase lo que se diga,
La ganó Mexicali; ahora falta el final
Que va a ser lo más sensacional.
Con relación al juego pasado,
Debemos confesar en honor
Del "team" derrotado,
Que jugó mucho mejor
Que el nuestro; pues si éste ganó
Fue porque así el Destino lo decretó...
Resultado: triunfaron los prietitos
(eso sí, con esfuerzos inauditos),
Con nueve carreras por dos.
¡Sea por Dios!

Se distinguieron Ramírez y Pujol
Terán. Arsenio y Agapito
Y sobre todos, Caballito:
"As" de "Ases" del "Base Ball",
Quien agarró un "home run"
Con tan "bona sorte"
Que la bola le dio un rozón
Al reloj de la Corte
Llevándose de paso las manecillas,
Y siguió de frente como catorce millas.
Un simpático americano
Que por cierto estaban en cuclillas,
(curioso incidente),
De su entusiasmo en los excesos,
Le dio a Cabal la mano
Y con la mano cinco pesos,
Que con tan noble fin
Se sacó el Míster de un calcetín.
En cambio, los de "Chinacal,"

Con abrazos y besos y gritos y ovaciones,
A falta de tostones,
Premiaron aquella jugada magistral
Del "Califa" Cabal.

Hubo este desagradable incidente;
Los señores jueces
No fueron del gusto, seguramente,
De los del Centro, siendo, como otras veces,
Personas honorables de su nacionalidad;
Y los cambiaron
Por otros que juzgaron
Obrarían con "menos imparcialidad."
No les valieron, pues, luchas ni ardides
Y no hubo más novedad.
Contra nuestros heroicos "Cides
Campeadores", a los centralenses:
Ni la cambiada de los jueces.
Ni la remuda de los lanzadores
Ni los palos "Cabal…lísticos"
Y exterminadores
Del Catcher coloso;
Nada pudo restar el estruendoso
Éxito de nuestros jugadores.

Bien por los triunfos conquistados
Por nuestros campeones denodados,
Que al fin vencieron su abulia
De tiempo pretéritos.
Aunque otros digan: "Gracias a la Julia"… *

Según todas las probabilidades
Vendrán en esta semana los chicagüenses
A jugar con los mexicalenses
Un match que será monumental,
Y que seguramente hará historia

Cuando menos en la memoria
De los pobladores del Valle Imperial.

Los "White Socks" ("Calcetines blancos")
De Chicago, tienen actualmente el control
De todos los torneos de "base ball"
Jugados en la Unión Americana,
De manera que si es verdad
Que vienen aquí esta semana
Los citados Maestros
A jugar con los Maestros
A jugar con los nuestros,
Ya podemos decir con orgullo
Y proclamarlo hasta en la calle

Que tenemos lo mejorcito del Valle.
A cada quien lo suyo.

Y aquí termino esta mal pergeñada
Nota. Que no es crónica ni nada.

* *Carro de la Ambulancia.*

Un buen golpe

El señor Inspector de Policía
Con dos o tres agentes
De esos que son la mera pulmonía
De tan inteligentes.
Y que por no pecar de negligentes
No duermen ni de noche ni de día.
De precauciones mil haciendo acopio
Encontró en cierta casa
Un fumadero de opio,
Y con todas las manos en la masa
A dos magnates chinos
De los más prominentes.
Y de los más cochinos;
(le suplicamos al lector que escupa).
Puesto que los hallaron chupa y chupa
Los citados agentes
Con la asquerosa pipa entre los dientes.
Y en tan grato ejercicio se quedara
Aquel par de mongoles
Entregándose al sucio
Vicio que tantos goces le depara,
Viendo quizá en sus sueños a Confucio
Bailando un "shimmy" con la "Theda-Bara".
Si el señor Inspector de Policía
Como dije primero
No los sacara de su fantasía
Para darles su pase al saladero,
O sea al Hotel Cota, al menos malo.
— Si he de decir verdad —
De la localidad.

Además de las pipas,
Según dice la gente
O la voz de la calle, que es lo propio,
En el tugurio chino

Se encontró lo siguiente:
Mil paquetes de opio
Entre corriente, regular y fino,
Y sobre blandos canapés, orquillas,
Peinetas, ligas y otras menesteres
Propios de las mujeres
Que usan la falda casi a las rodillas.
Un archivo completo con la historia
De los grandes negocios
Que explotan ciertos socios
Cuyo nombre se escapa a mi memoria.
Item más: una guía
Para el cultivo de la adormidera
Y de la marihuana,
Y un plan para atraer en pleno día
La droga que se quiera
Sin miedo a los espías de la Aduana.
El golpe, dado, pues, a los viciosos
Y a los explotadores
De la droga asesina,
Que hoy salir no pudieron victoriosos
Como en tiempos mejores
Porque ya no hay "combina"...
(perdonen esta frase los lectores),
Sienta un buen precedente
Y, es, naturalmente,
Un eficaz remedio
En la higienización de nuestro medio.

Bien por el Inspector de Policía
Que no mira en el vicio
Algo de su provecho y beneficio.
Tal y como se hacía
"allá en un tiempo cuando Dios quería"...

Abril 10 de 1922
Mexicali, B.C.

Una sesión borrascosa

En la sesión del "ache" Ayuntamiento
Del viernes retropróximo,
Jugaron los ediles de la izquierda
El todo por el todo,
A fin de destituir al Presidente
Por la cuestión del opio
Y la morfina, que según decían,
Se dijo que dijeron que había dicho
Los rumores del "pópulo."

Yo no voy a poner de mi cosecha
En caso tan penoso,
Un solo grano: quiero solamente
Pintarles a mi modo
Pero sujeto a la verdad histórica
El papel poco airoso
De los señores Regidores que hacen
Del Cuerpo...cuasi-autónomo,
Un herradero digno de individuos
Sin juicio y sin decoro.

La sesión queda abierta. Son las cinco,
No falta ni uno solo
De los ediles.
Lee el Secretario
El acta. Su monótono
Acento hace pensar en el zumbido
De un moscón perezoso.
Rosas medita, Chávez ronronea,
Y Luego piensa un poco,
Ronca Roncal y Ríos se sonríe,
Y entrecierra los ojos,
Como quien va a pescar en el espacio;
Rodríguez está hosco:
El público entre tanto desespera;

Pero surge de pronto
La voz del Regidor al fin citado
Quien pide con buen modo
Se cambien ciertas frases que no dijo
El viernes retropróximo;
Luego "lecha" le viga al Secretario
Y también a don Otto;
Pero al quedar el acta corregida
Se calman los enojos.
Siguen varios asuntos: el degüello,
Del chivo, (no expiatorio)
Que mató don Golías, y el marrano
Que ajustició don Lolo;
Los árboles que obstruyen los canales
No recuerdo en qué rancho,
Y que están inclinados hacia dentro
O hacia fuera...(¡qué diablo!)
Sin querer he cambiado el asonante,
Lo cual me importa un rábano);
La balanza de libras recogida
A un pobre campirano,
En la cual, según dice, sólo pesa
A sus quince chamacos;
La renuncia de Iribe y el recurso
Del simpático Pancho
Que solicita el "hueso" luego, luego,
Si no, ¿pa qué peleamos?;
Las dietas del Consejo de Electores:
 (unos seis pesos diarios),
Y otros asuntos mil que finalizan
Como a las diez y cuarto.
(Y luego se dirá que los ediles
No desquitan el "jando.")

Por fin suena la hora tan deseada
De los papirotazos.
Toca su turno desgraciadamente

A los pobres empleados
A quienes por razón de economía
Se acortan los salarios,
Sin incluir, por supuesto, al Presidente,
Ni a otros funcionarios
De los que ganan muchos tecolines
Porque...saben ganarlos.
Se suprime también la policía
Privada, tras de un rato
De discusión, y la especial escapa
Al supremo escobazo;
Y después de defensa tan brillante
A favor del Erario,
Como vienen después de la tormenta
Los truenos y los rayos,
Y en torrentes desátase la lluvia
En el estéril llano,
Así Lugo Rodríguez se desatan
Contra Moller el cándido,
Quien, según aseguraran sus amigos,
Quebrar no sabe un plato;
Le dicen que la ley es soberana,
Que el artículo tantos
De la Constitución del 17
Ha sido conculcado;
Que Reyes no es edil, que a Manuel Díaz
Lo encontraron cuidando
A varios jugadores siendo agente
Del cuerpo policíaco;
Que Moller dijo un día que decían
Que era puro germano,
Y en resumen, que para Presidente
Les venía muy guango.
Moller replica a nuestros dos ediles
En un tono más agrio,
Que mientras no le prueben lo que dicen
Están desprestigiando

Al "muy ache" Cabildo; que se callen
Porque de lo contrario
El público creerá que allí se trata
De una plaza de gallos.

Eran las doce en punto de la noche
(o sean las veinticuatro),
Cuando, del auditorio por fortuna,
Terminó el espectáculo.

Ojalá y el lector cuando aquí llegue
Si llega por acaso,
Al leer este informe soporífero,
No me despache al diablo.

Mayo de 1922
Mexicali, B.C.

Un triunfo clamoroso

Para ensalzar la póstuma victoria
Que obtuvieron los nuestros
En el último juego de la Liga,
¡oh Musa del Base Ball!, prestadme aliento;
Dadme el estro divino
Del inmortal Homero;
Prestadme las trompetas de la Fama
Para hacerle saber al mundo entero
Que en el Valle Imperial no hubo partido
Que al mexicano le tomara el pelo;
Que a pesar de las trampas y chanchullos
Que los jueces hicieron
Y de ser nuestros pobres pelotaris
Tan feos y tan prietos
(no lo digo por Buiti ni el Corúa.
Por Agapito, menos);
Ganaron la victoria. Ahora invito
A los de Mexicali y los de El Centro.
Que al terminar la brega,
Como buenos vecinos y apareceros
Griten cogidos todos de la mano:
¡Bravo por Mexicali! ¡Viva El Centro!

El juego va a empezar. En los tendidos
Hay un número inmenso
De espectadores, y los autos llegan
A más de cuatrocientos.

Conforme al Reglamento respectivo,
Van al palo los nuestros;
Los contrarios se aprestan a la lucha.
El **pitcher** en su puesto.
El **catcher** y el **umpire** se acomodan
Los bélicos arreos.

Buiti en el **bat,** y los mexicalenses
Hablando por los codos y codos...

Primer Inc.: un punto Mexicali.
Segundo: una carrera para El Centro.
Tercero: Calavera a calavera
Y siguen... es aquel un cementerio
Hasta el sexto en que anotan los contrarios
Un punto más por otro de los nuestros.

Ninguno de los dos logra hacer nada
En el siguiente encuentro.
En el octavo, Mexicali nada
Y un punto más El Centro.
Tres por dos a favor de los vecinos
Marca el "score"; los nuestros
Van a jugar el todo por el todo
En el "ining" noveno.

Los rostros palidecen. En las gradas
Los "paisanos" suspenden el aliento,
Y se oyera volar si alas tuviese
Hasta el mismo silencio.

El Corúa va al palo, y ¡zaz! Atiza
Un "hit"; llega a primero
Mientras Ramírez con igual fortuna
De aquel sigue el ejemplo,
Tomando la inicial que le ha dejado
Libre su compañero.

Sigue Terán. Tres bolas, dos "estraiques"
Y logran un "hit" soberbio
Hasta segunda base,
Entrando victoriosos los primeros.
Buitti en el bat, ¡cuidado!
Viene el lance supremo.

Tira el "pitcher" la bola, y con la fuerza
Con que lanza la nube de su seno
El rayo, Buiti, al golpe del garrote
Lanza la bola y corre y... vuelta al ruedo.

Todos los compatriotas
Se alzan de sus asientos,
Gritan, aplauden, saltan, gesticulan
Y lanzan por el aire sus sombreros.

Muchos llegan al campo, a Buiti abrazan
Otros hacen pucheros
Y besan al coloso de la tarde.
Mientras tanto, uno de ellos
Colecta algunos dólares,
Cuarenta más o menos
Que ofrece al short-stop en testimonio
De admiración y afecto.
Un Míster, en un rato de entusiasmo
Le obsequia cinco pesos.
Se calman los espíritus un tanto
Y continúa el juego:
Dos puntos más para los triunfadores
Y los contrarios, Cero.

Resumen: seis carreras Mexicali
Por sólo tres de El Centro.

Acá entre nos, a Buiti
Quemóse mucho incienso
Y se olvidó a Terán, a cuyo empuje
Sin duda se debieron
Los puntos de Ramírez y Corúa
Con los cuales ganado estaba el juego;
Sin quitarle al "home run" de Buitemea
Su verdadero mérito.

Como siempre, Agapito, formidable;
Cabal en el tercero
Cogiendo la pelota hasta en las nubes;
Ramírez tuvo un juego
Magnífico. Los fielders, regulares;
Terancito y Arsenio
Dignos de figurar en las novenas...
De los santos del cielo.

Los jueces muy parciales: a los suyos
Siempre en los fallos la razón les dieron,
Lo cual no es de extrañarse:
Estaban en su puesto.
Que por primera vez dice El Examiner
Comentando los juegos
De la liga, conquista el campeonato
Un país extranjero.

¡Olé por los inditos!
¡Qué honra para México...!

Abril de 1921
Mexicali, B.C.

Los vecinos de Mexicali

Los vecinos de Mexicali
Están que no caben de gusto,
Por los dos últimos proyectos
Del señor Gobernador Lugo.
El primero va encaminado
A mejorar el servicio espurio
Del agua, que como sabemos
Es absolutamente nulo;
Pues algunos barrios carecen
De él porque no sirven los tubos
Y la presión es poca, y es mucha
El calor por aquellos rumbos.
Para que el proyecto no quede
En promesa, como otros muchos
Que los pasados Gobernantes
Ofrecieron, el señor Lugo
Exhibió el costo de un tanque
De cien mil galones, y pudo
Firmar el contrato del caso
Y sin despilfarro ninguno.
El otro proyecto en cuestión
Es el de una planta de luz
Eléctrica; pues la que padecen
Aquellos infelices es muy
Deficiente: cara y muy mala,
Porque los empresarios, ¡Jesús!
Sólo tratan de enriquecerse:
Desvalijan al pueblo y...!abúr!...
Ya se piden proposiciones
A nacionales y a extranjeros
Sobre bases equitativas
Para encausar este proyecto,
Dándosele la preferencia
A aquel que cobre menos,
Y en igualdad de condiciones

A un mexicano. Ya tendremos
Pues, luz y agua en Mexicali
Sin traerla desde Calexico
Que amablemente nos la brinda
A cambio de nuestro dinero...
Van a realizarse por fin
Las promesas de los eternos
Directores de la política
Que tantas veces ofrecieron
Agua, luz y tierras baratas
En las elecciones, al pueblo,
Con la intención de encaramarse
En el poder por esos medios.

Miren ustedes: francamente
Como buen mexicano me alegro
Por las mejoras materiales
Que anotadas arriba dejo,
Pero se me parte el corazón
Al considerar los esfuerzos
De los pobrecitos políticos
Parásitos del presupuesto,
Por buscar para sus programas
Otros mejores elementos;
Pues gracias al Gobernador
Lugo, luz y agua ya tendremos.

Junio de 1922
Mexicali, B.C.

Carnaval en Mexicali

Bajo muy buenos auspicios
Se ha iniciado el Carnaval,
Que resultará suntuoso
Y espléndido a no dudar,
Más que en años anteriores,
Gracias a la actividad
Desplegada por las damas
Que integran ahora el Gran
Comité Organizador
De Festejos. Ellas han
Organizado tardeadas
Que resultan, en verdad,
Hermosas fiestas sociales,
Y quedó iniciado ya
El Concurso para Reina
Del próximo Carnaval;
Obteniendo Belem Vega
Que es una divinidad,
Quinientos votos, y Elena
Urroz, (hurí celestial),
Ciento cincuenta; y se espera
Que de cien mil pasarán
Los sufragios emitidos.
Hay una barbaridad
De entusiasmo por saber
Quién victoriosa saldrá
Del torneo. Ya don Víctor
Carusso, el mero Rajá
De la esplendidez, ha dicho
— Y no se raja, — que va
A ponerle la corona
De la Regencia a la más
Popular mexicalense.
(Ya veremos si es verdad).
Por su parte el Comité,

En el que figuran las
Más distinguidas damitas
De la mejor sociedad,
México-calexiquense,
Que con tanta habilidad
Dirige Laurita R.
De Ulloa, sin descansar
Trabaja porque las fiestas
Del futuro Carnaval
Constituyan una espléndida
Y hermosa nota social.
Muy pronto publicaremos
La efigie de la beldad
Que cada sábado obtenga
Más sufragios, sin faltar
La lista de candidatas,
(un florecido rosal),
Que en este regio Concurso
Figuren hasta el final.

Febrero de 1923
Mexicali, B.C.

Las elecciones

Pasaron las elecciones
Del muy Ilustre Cabildo,
Como pasan las películas
Por la pantalla: sin ruido.
Hubo algunos "protestantes"
En contra de actos indignos
Que se arrojaron al rostro
Mutuamente los partidos:
Que se negaron boletas
En tres o cuatro Distritos
A ciudadanos conscientes
Porque no eran del "circuito":
Pero que, en cambio, en los otros
Votaron hasta los niños.

Resultado: que según
Los "Rojos y Campesinos",
Ellos salieron triunfantes,
Y los del otro partido:
— el Club Nacional del Pueblo —
Nos aseguran lo mismo.

Ya veremos en la junta
Del Honorable Cabildo
Que se efectuará el primero
Del año, el fin de este lío.

Por el "Edén"

El cuadro Arte Nuevo
Que trae Chacel,
Debuta el domingo
En el teatro "Edén";
Se trae un elenco
Que... allá solo él
Puede saber cómo
Hacerlo tan bien...
Viene Ernesto Rubio,
Un tenor chipén
De esos que conmueven
Los cimientos del
Teatro donde actúan
Y el techo también,
(si no, que lo diga
Nuestro teatro "Edén".)
Viene Teté Tapia,
— la divina Esther —,
Una actriz que marcha
Con arte y con fe
Camino a la Gloria,
¡Bravo por Teté!
La bella Carmela
Que al mover los pies,
Hace que los ángeles,
— y hasta San José —
Se asomen al cielo
Y griten ¡olé!

Y se sigue en turno
La señora Areu,
Que caracteriza
Sus tipos muy bien;
Y la dama joven:

La niña Chacel,
Un primor de artista
Que no hay más que ver.

Entre el masculino
Elemento, tres
Son los que descuellan:
El propio Chacel,
¡(Claro! El Director),
Molgosa y Pepet,
Todos, veteranos
De la escena, pues...

En cambio nos faltan
Coristas: son tres
Ellas y dos ellos,
Y como se ve,
Con un coro así
No se sale bien
En obras que exigen
Algo en el "retén".
A Rubio, el tenor
Le falta algo de
Vocalización,
Y le sobra en
Ciertos calderones
La vez a granel.

Y...con mis excusas,
La linda Té-Té,
Como tiple... canta;
Pero ese no es
Su fuerte. Lo dije
E insisto otra vez:
La Gloria la espera
Por la escala que
Ascendiera Sara

Bernard, y otras cien
Actrices de fama
Mundial. ¿Dije bien?
Y basta por hoy.
Ya me ocuparé
Detenidamente,
Un poco después,
Del Cuadro Moderno
Que trae Chacel.

Diciembre 13 de 1922
Mexicali, B.C.

Míster BLIND

El pacto del silencio

Los ilustres miembros
Del cuerpo edilicio,
De un santo derecho
En pleno ejercicio,

Firmaron un pacto
Que todo concilia:
Desde los "recuerdos"
Para la familia

Hasta el muy castizo:
"No sea usté hablador".
Y llaman al pacto
"Un Pacto de Honor"

El cual los obliga
Sólo moralmente
A obrar en las juntas
De modo prudente.

¿Qué Rosas y Castro
Ya por la costumbre
"Tiran el sarape"
Y están que echan lumbre?

Inmediatamente
Y con gesto airado
Loera les recuerda
El pacto firmado.

¿Qué Ángeles y Mérida
Truenan? En el acto
Algún compañero
Les recuerda el pacto.

Y de esta manera
Tan llana y sencilla
El Muy Honorable
Marcha a maravilla

Sin que yo averigüe
Si en el fondo de esto,
Para ciertos líos
Sólo hay un pretexto...

Ni si los ediles
Dejaron sus viejas
Cuitas porque temen
Un jalón de orejas

De Papá Gobierno,
Que el orden procura
Y a los que alborotan
Los mete en cintura.

Es de enviarles una
Felicitación,
A los consejales
Por su conversión...

Ojalá no pase
En cualquier mal rato
Lo del que tenía
Los ojos de gato,

Quien, por una rara
Y fuerte atracción,
Se le iban los ojos
Al ver un ratón...

Marzo de 1923.
Mexicali, B.C.

Míster BLIND

Los filibusteros

Los Filibusteros
De allende la "cerca",
Están lamentando
Su conducta puerca
Que los extravía
Por negros senderos.
¡Cómo me dan lástima
Los filibusteros!...

¡Pobres huerfanitos!
Aunque no les cuadre
Debemos decirles
Que no tienen madre;
Y si aún la tienen,
¡infeliz mujer!
Mejor le valiera
No verlos nacer,

Que considerarlos
Traidores y arteros.
¡Cómo me dan lástima
Los filibusteros!...

Y si el hambre guíalos
Hacia la traición,
Entonces me causan
Más que compasión...
¡Pobres! Azuzados
Por los altos "Jefes"
Que ven en aquellos
Simples mequetrefes,
Viles instrumentos
De su fementida
Labor, mientras ellos
Se dan la gran vida;

Judas que se venden
Por treinta dineros...
¡Cómo me dan lástima
Los filibusteros!...

Invadir soñaron
El Distrito Norte;
Pero no contaron
Con el "pasaporte"...
Y ahora lamentan
En extraño léxico
Su fracaso. ¡Pobres!
Sufren en Calexico
El desprecio, hasta
De los extranjeros.
¡Cómo me dan lástima
Los filibusteros!...

Octubre de 1922
Mexicali, B.C.

La ciudad abierta

A las primeras "chispas
De la mañana,
Salí de Mexicali
Para Tijuana
Por la vía más corta:
La serranía
Que allá nos lleva en menos
De medio día,
Cuando hacemos el viaje
Con buena suerte,
O lo que da lo mismo,
Cuando la muerte
No asoma su silueta
Por los barrancos
Que bordean el camino
Por ambos flancos,
En cuyo negro fondo
Los automóviles
Con chofer y pasaje
Quedan inmóviles.

¡San Diego! ¡Hermoso puerto!
Ciudad gemela
De todas las de Estados
Unidos. Hela
Ahí con sus hoteles,
Altos, muy altos,
Sus parques, sus tranvías
Y sus asfaltos,
Sus calles numeradas:
La principal:
(Main Street,) y sus teatros
Con nombre igual
Que en otras poblaciones.
La tienda "Kress",

La "Sole Service" y la
De "Cinco y Diez."

La mañana siguiente
Dejé a San Diego,
Arribando a Tijuana,
Luego, tan luego,
Que al correr del "Fordcito"
En media hora
Estaba en la "Cosmópolis"
Pecadora;
Dos cuadras de burdeles
Y de cantinas
Y cabarets, en donde
Las mesalinas
Con mil artes atraen
A la clientela,
Bailan semidesnudas,
Beben y "pelan"
A los tontos que caen
Bajo sus redes.
(Por si acaso lo ignoran,
Sépanlo ustedes).
Es de verse los sábados
Y los domingos
A Tijuana repleta
De puros "gringos",
Que con sus respectivas
Acompañantes
Quieren probarnos que ellos
Son "temperantes"
Y en amable consorcio
Con los nativos
Toman sus "inocentes"
Aperitivos,
Hasta que los rubores
De la mañana

Caen piadosamente
Sobre Tijuana.

El curioso turista
Que sólo viene
A observar las costumbres
Y que no tiene
Para qué amanecerse
Vase temprano
A dormir a su cuarto,
Pero es en vano:
Apenas duerme un poco
Luego despierta
A los golpes brutales
Que da en la puerta
Un Míster que masculla:
— "abre Juanita",
Y usted se desespera,
Brama y se irrita;
Pero con un "excuse me"
De aquel intruso
Queda todo arreglado.
¡Vaya un abuso!...
Se duerme usted de nuevo
Y en la vecina
Estancia oye usted una
Voz femenina
Que grita: ¡sinvergüenza!
Y un golpe seco,
Se asoma, y ve que un hombre
Sale en chaleco...
Por fin, como a las cuatro
De la mañana,
Y cuando ya los ruidos
Hanse calmado,
Duerme usted un instante y...
¡suerte tirana!

¡dos gatos se enamoran
En el tejado!...
Por lo demás, Tijuana,
Ciudad abierta
Que los vicios y al dólar
Brinda su puerta,
Y al Erario coloca
Alto, muy alto,
No tiene agua, banquetas,
Ni luz ni asfalto,
Ni drenaje, ni rastro...
¡no tiene nada!
Porque los fondos todos
Van a Ensenada,
Y ahí se distribuyen
"de tal manera"
Que a Tijuana "le cantan
La firulera"...

Julio 11 de 1921
Tijuana, B.C.

Salvemos de la horca a un hermano

Al pie del patíbulo.
Está un compatriota,
Un hermano nuestro
Que en maldita hora
A matar lo obligan
En defensa propia.
El caso fue éste:
Aureliano Pompa,
Joven emigrado
Vino de Sonora
A buscar trabajo
A esta Babilonia
Pues como otros muchos
Creyó en las historias
De los buenos sueldos
Y las pocas horas
De labor, y en tantas
Cosas ilusorias.

Extraño en el medio
Y sin el idioma,
Solo de peón pudo
Trabajar. Con toda
Constancia se entrega
A la lucha; arrostra
Mil visicitudes,
Pero al cabo logra
Realizar su anhelo,
Su ilusión más honda:
Mandar a los suyos
Unos cuantos dólares
El paño de lágrimas
Para sus congojas.
Mas…sobre la vida
De Aureliano Pompa

Se proyecta un día
Una marcha roja:
Recibe un ultraje
Nuestro compatriota,
Le golpea el rostro
Un capataz; otra
Y otra vez lo ultraja,
Y por fin lo acosa
Empuñando un marro.
Al ver esto, Pompa
Retrocede y saca
Presto su pistola
Y dispara y mata
En defensa propia.
Cuentan así el caso
No pocas personas
Que lo presenciaron:
Sin embargo, a Pompa
La justicia quiere
Llevarlo a la horca.

Primero "El Heraldo"
Y la prensa toda
Después, (en justicia
Digámoslo ahora,)
Abren la campaña
De defensa y logran
Que envíen su óbolo
Nuestros compatriotas.
Varios abogados
A su cargo toman
La defensa, y luchan
De manera heroica
Por salvar la vida
A Aureliano Pompa.
Ayudemos todos
En cualquiera forma

A tan noble empresa:
Salvar de la horca
A un hermano nuestro,
A ese compatriota
Que espera en su celda
La última hora.

Salvar del martirio
A una pobre madre
Que en silencio llora,
Que por el ausente
Suspira y solloza;
Que siente las ansias
De la misma muerte
Pensando en la horca,
Pensando en su hijo,
(¡Mater Dolorosa!)
Y que tal vez no tenga el consuelo
De besarlo en su última hora...

AYUDEMOS TODOS
A AURELIANO POMPA.

Marzo 31 de 1923
Mexicali, B.C.

TERCERA PARTE

Corrida de toros

La corrida del último domingo
Según las opiniones
Que por ahí distingo,
Muy aceptable fue, por lo que toca
Al ganado, que en malas condiciones
Y un tanto estropeado
Por natural efecto del camino,
Como pudo cumplió con su destino...
Los mimados del público: Torquito
Y Rivera, a la altura de su fama;
Aquel con el primero,
Y éste con el segundo
Lograron poco en capa y banderillas.
Torquito, muleteando, muy certero
Y con la espada haciendo maravillas;
Pues despachó ese toro y el tercero
De una sola estocada,
(a cada uno, se entiende),
En la parte indicada.
Rivera con los trastos de la muerte
En su toro segundo
Tuvo tan mala suerte
Por culpa del astado,
— Pues se movía de uno y otro lado —,
Que dio varios pinchazos
A aquel semi-novillo,
Piquetes y arañazos;
Acertándole al fin en el codillo
Golpe tan furibundo,
Que se fue al otro mundo
Con una "horrible frase" en el morrillo.
Apenas sale "Guerra", el mulillero,
Arrastrando al rumiante,
Cuando se abre la puerta del chiquero,
Y aparece, arrogante

Y con poder bastante
Para embestir al universo entero,
El último cornudo de la tarde
Que por su hermosa estampa es el primero.
Los tendidos aclaman a la fiera;
Coge Pérez Rivera
La capa, y nos engarza
Faroles y verónicas
Dignos de cien mil crónicas,
Y Torquito se "alza"
Y toma la franela
Y nos brinda la flor de la canela.
Se trae al enemigo
Envuelto entre los pliegues de la carpa,
Totalmente lo empapa
Veroniqueando; le acaricia al reo
Los pitones, y sigue en el floreo
Entre dianas, y gritos y ovaciones,
Que oyen ambos toreros
Viendo a sus pies cachuchas y sombreros.
(entre ellos un kepí de los bomberos),
Puros, cigarros, dulces y tostones...
En banderillas se repite el acto;
Parece que hacen pacto
De lucir sus arrestos
Los dos citados diestros;
Pues a un par de Rivera
Que el Gran Belmonte para si quisiera,
Sigue otro de Torquito
Que la obra corona,
Digno del Gran Gaona!...
(Echar mano del símil necesito.)
Tocan a muerte; coge la muleta
Pérez Rivera. Un pase natural,
Otro ayudado por debajo, otro
Peinando al animal; uno de pecho;
Un pase de rodillas... ¡Colosal!

Que al joven matador le viene estrecho.
Y la vida se juega
En los morros del bicho;
Pero el momento llega
En que éste pague cara su bravura
Y su raro capricho
De ostentar tan bellísima figura.
Coge el niño el estoque,
Se perfila, un pinchazo y... ¡el disloque!
¡El acero en la cruz! Nueva faena;
Firme el brazo y a fondo... ¡hasta la bola!
El herido burel se descontrola
Y rueda hecho papilla por la arena
Muerto desde el testuz hasta la cola!...
Y por si aún le queda algún resuello,
Rivera le receta el descabello.
Los músicos, el público y...los toros
Que en el corral escuchan la algaraza
Y adivinan la suerte,
Tocan, gritan y braman, a la muerte
Del último en señal de regocijo,
(cada quien en su "idioma", bien se advierte),
— El mismo sol — un español nos dijo —
Suspende su carrera
Y llora de placer viendo a Rivera
Como si fuese su hijo.
(Claro ¡Como que el sol
Antes que Astro y que Rey es...español.)
El Carbonero Grande y Gaonita
Quedaron bien; Limeño a gran altura,
Hizo buena figura.
La pica... ¡esa no se necesita!
Entrada: buena en sol!, en sombra poca.
El público contento;
Y aquí se acaba el cuento.
Punto en boca.

Marzo de 1923
Mexicali, B.C.

El cartepillar
(El Gusano de Venice)

En las playas de Venecia
Como en todos los demás
Balnearios de moda, vemos
Una inmensa variedad
De diversiones. Cada año
Los que las explotan, traen
Algo nuevo para el público
Que en gran romería va
A disfrutar de los dulces
Atractivos del "gud taim",
O a recibir las caricias
Y la sonrisa del mar.

En el presente verano
Encontramos, además
De la "montaña", y la "Casa
De Locos", y el infernal
Paseo de las canastas
Que sacuden sin cesar
El cuerpo, como arrastradas
Por el mismo Satanás,
Y el hipódromo, en que vemos
A las mayores de edad
Confundidas con las niñas,
A horcajadas sobre "Sam"
O "John", (llevan los caballos
Estos nombres y otros más),
Encantadoras criaturas,
"Amazonas del Ideal"...
Cuya falta flota al viento
Como estandarte triunfal...
Además de todas estas
Diversiones, (otras hay
Encontramos, digno, ahora,

Una muy original):
Se trata de un "Cartepillar"
(Gusano), ("cartepilar"
Apochando la palabra),
Gigantesco, en el que van
Los pasajeros en coches
Con toda comodidad.
El dicho animal afecta
Una forma circular
Con diámetro de unos quince
Pies poco menos o más,
Y evoluciona al conjuro
De un mecanismo especial.
Deseando estudiar de cerca
El raro "cartepilar",
Con otras muchas personas
Me llegué hacia el animal,
Colocándose a la vera
(pícara casualidad),
De una linda paisanita,
De las que vienen de "allá".

Comienza a andar el gusano
En su forma irregular,
Y mientras corre, nos cubre
Poco a poco, con su gran
Caparazón, — si se admite —,
Imitando, en realidad,
Un gusano gigantesco
En carrera circular,
El cual nos deja, al correr,
En completa obscuridad,
Y entre cortinas espesas...
(¡Virgen de la Soledad!)
Que separan cada coche;
Y luego un viento tenaz

Sopla de abajo hacia arriba
Con insistente crueldad...

La ilusión dura muy poco...
Cesa la velocidad
Del anillado vehículo,
Y lentamente se va
Levantando el carapacho
y...paremos de contar.

Me despido de mi dama
Con un saludo especial,
Salgo y tropiezo con una
Persona de mi amistad
Que me dice muy bajito
Y en tono confidencial:
Ya que pintas los labios
Pon más cuidado, pues traes
Pintura hasta la nariz,
Hombre, ¡qué barbaridad...
(Lo mismo les pasa a muertos
Que van al "cartepillar.")

Ahí tienen los lectores
La última novedad
Con que pasan las parejas
Un magnifico "gud taim".

Junio de 1923
Los Angeles, Calif.

Míster BLIND

En defensa de la Phillips

El viernes trajeron
De Tegucigalpa
A la Clara Phillips,
La mujer más mala
Que haya visto el mundo
En la Era Cristiana...
Todos la condenan,
Todos la maltratan
En su fuero interno,
Y arrojan montañas
De odio sobre ella,
Más aún las damas
Que imploran Justicia
Y claman venganza.
Nadie compadece
A la desgraciada
Que amó con delirio,
Que sintió en su alma
De los negros celos
El soplo que mata.
Su inmenso cariño
Vio que la robaban,
Y como no tienen
Pena señalada
En las leyes nuestras
Los ladrones de almas,
Ella, enloquecida
Ante su desgracia,
Como la tigresa
A quien arrebatan
Sus cachorros, ruge,
Y clava las garras.
¿Qué cínicamente
Confiesa su falta?
¿Que no se arrepiente?

¿Que no tienen entrañas?
¿Que ante la Justicia
Se sonríe impávida?
¡Quién sabe qué luchas
Sostiene en su ánima!...

No disculpo el crimen:
La Justicia Humana
Debe corregirlo;
Pues si se dejara
Impune, sería
Tal vez peor desgracia.
¡Pero acaso el hombre
Puede, en su ignorancia
De los infinitos
Misterios del alma,
Con sólo sus códigos
Juzgar al que mata?

Junio de 1923
Mexicali, B.C.

Míster BLIND

El divorcio

Las gentes de este país
Progresista y laborioso,
Donde todo se traduce
A tanto más cuanto en oro,
No ven como en otras partes
En el santo matrimonio
El lazo que une a las almas
Por "sécula seculorum".
Aquí la dulce coyunda
Es como cualquier negocio,
Salvo honrosas excepciones,
Que debe haberlas en todo.

Convienen en ver al Juez
Los pretensos, y sin otros
Arreglos preliminares
Ultiman el matrimonio,
Como firman un contrato
En una empresa dos socios.

¿Qué las cosas andan mal?
Es decir, que los esposos
No se avienen? Se liquida
Incontinenti el negocio,
O lo que da igual; acuerden
Ambas partes el divorcio.

Son infinitos los casos
En que se deshace el moño
Conyugal por obra y gracia
De las leyes del divorcio.
Generalmente lo piden
Las mujeres. ¿Que el esposo
Estornuda muy seguido
Por la noche? ¡Escandaloso!

Es cosa de ver al Juez
Y de pedir el divorcio.

¿Que la mujer, por capricho
Tiene perrito, y que el otro,
Digo, el marido, no puede
Soportar el alboroto
Que arma el chucho a cada paso?
Pues... a pedir el divorcio.
Que el pobre marido compra
Un sombrero "muy lujoso"
De dos pesos, sin la venia
De su mujer? Qué piropos
Recibe aquel desgraciado
Por bribón y manirroto;
¡Dizque gastarse dos pesos
En un sombrero! ¡Es el colmo!
Y, de nuevo el estribillo:
Hay que pedir el divorcio.

Otras muchas se separan
Porque el marido es muy corto
Y no llena la medida
De su ingenio caprichoso;
Y la más... por divorciarse
Y buscar uno a su antojo.

Por fortuna ya la ley
Tiende a restringir un poco,
Para bien de la moral
Los motivos del divorcio,
Y algunas damas laboran
Con afán digno de encomio,
Por "higienizar" el medio,
Para que se vea pronto
Más amor en los hogares,
Más respeto al matrimonio.

Para cooperar al noble
Proyecto, yo les propongo,
Ya que la fiebre del "record"
Se ha filtrado aquí tan hondo,
Una encuesta nunca vista:
La ENCUESTA DEL MATRIMONIO
CONTINUO, con un Gran Premio
Al que tenga más retoños.

Junio de 1923
Los Angeles, Calif.

La sucesión presidencial

Nuestros políticos
Comienzan ya
A prepararse
Para la gran
Campaña próxima
Presidencial;
Y ya se sabe
De tres o más
Presidenciales;
Pero no hay
Ningún partido
Que lance a
Su candidato,
¿Por qué será?
Unos señalan
Al General
Calles, (y conste
Que son los más),
Como el más viable,
Otros están
Por de la Huerta,
Hombre capaz,
Muy honorable,
Muy popular,
Pero que ha dicho
Sin vacilar
Desde Hermosillo
Que no entrará
A la campaña
Presidencial.
Los agraristas
Quieren lanzar
A Soto y Gama
El radical;
Los profesores

Todos están
Con Vasconcelos
¿Y los demás?
Los clericales
Color no dan
Pero trabajan
Sin descansar
Por imponernos
Su voluntad,
Y a tal efecto
Se reunirán,
En la metrópoli,
Mas sin lograr
Lo que pretenden
Con tanto afán.
Los reaccionarios
Quieren sacar
También las uñas,
Y tienen ya
Su candidato:
El general
Don Félix Díaz,
Quien correrá...
(ni el más ligero
Lo va a alcanzar),
Como aspirante,
(una vez más?)
En la campaña
Presidencial.

Ningún partido
He dicho mal,
Hase lanzado
Con voluntad
A la campaña
Franca y leal,
Y necesito

Rectificar:
En Mexicali
El "Nacional
Cooperatista"
Designó ya
Su candidato:
El General
Calles, el hombre
Que, a no dudar,
En el concepto
De Míster Blind
Y en el de todo
Buen liberal
Si a triunfar llega,
Continuará
La obra patriótica
Del Jefe actual.

Junio de 1923
Los Angeles, Calif.

Míster BLIND

México en caricatura

En un teatro de la Broadway
"de cuyo nombre no quiero
Acordarme," se denigra
A nuestro querido México.
"On the Border" se titula
Un mamarracho grosero
Que representa ahí
Tres o cuatro majaderos,
Escrito con las pezuñas
Por algún "húmedo" de esos
Que van a nuestra frontera
Porque aquí todo está seco,
Y en cabarets y cantinas
Pletóricos de extranjeros
Guardan el Domingo azul...
Brindando a Baco y a Venus;
Y que regresan después
Renegando de lo nuestro.

Aparece en el tablado
La garita de Calexico
Frente a la de Mexicali,
(así lo colijo al menos
A juzgar por las cantinas
Que se miran a lo lejos
Y junto a la "línea.") En está
El consabido crucero
Que reza: "Estados Unidos,"
De un lado, y del otro, "México."

Sale a escena el que parece
Jefe del Resguardo nuestro:
(Un ciudadano honorable,
Acá entre nos, el auténtico),
Ostentando en color verde

Una chaqueta de cuero,
El chaleco blanco, y rojo
El pantalón, esto es: México;
Sombrero charro, y al hombro
Dos carabinas; al "tiento"
La daga. Si se pudiese
Fulminar con el deseo
Autor y protagonista
Habrían volado muy lejos.

Y vienen otras escenas
Que ponen al rojo negro
Nuestra indignación, las cuales
Nos callamos por respeto
Al público que nos lee.

Ojalá el Cónsul de México
En esta ciudad se entere
Del caso y ponga el remedio.
Mientras tanto, la Colonia
Mexicana, y aun los miembros
De la hispano-americana,
Por dignidad, no debemos
Patrocinar una empresa
Que así denigra lo nuestro,
Y que pretende violar
Los sacratísimos fueros
Y el honor de un pueblo libre,
Que se merece el respeto
De los países más grandes
Y cultos del Universo.

Mayo de 1923
Los Angeles, Calif.

Míster BLIND

México auténtico

Debutó en el "Auditorium",
El teatro más elegante
Entre los mejores teatros
De la ciudad de Los Ángeles,
(por algo lo eligen todas
Las altas celebridades),
El cuadro *México auténtico*
Que nos trae Nelly Fernández:
Un cuadro muy mexicano
De artistas de pura sangre
Cuya lema es: "Por la Raza,
Por la Patria y por el Arte".

Ya la prensa mexicana
Y los periódicos yanquis
Hicieron justos elogios
De nuestros paisanos; y antes
De seguir su jira a Europa,
Permítanme dedicarles
Estos pobres "palos" míos
Que de lo íntimo nacen.

El Maestro Cantú inicia
El programa de la tarde
Bajo su sabia batuta
Con los "Aires Nacionales",
Esa música vernácula
Que en su divino lenguaje
Nos habla de las tristezas
De una Raza de Titanes.
Nelly, la graciosa Nelly,
Canzonetista admirable
Que nos brinda en sus canciones
Las brisas de nuestros valles
Y el rocío diamantino

Que brilla entre los rosales,
Nelly, el alma de la "troupe":
Juventud, Belleza y Arte,
Nos presenta bailes típicos,
(Entre otros, el Jarabe
Tapatío, y "La Sandunga")
Que en su traje de carácter
Ejecuta todo el cuadro
Con maestría inimitable.

Isabel Zenteno canta,
Y su voz cálida y suave,
Voz de soprano dramática
De dulces sonoridades,
Nos hace sentir muy hondo
Las romanzas nacionales.

"El que Calla Otorga". Poema
Por don Ernesto Finance,
Declamado por él mismo,
Quien viste el típico traje
Del chinampero. Nos dice
En sus pintorescas frases
Que la Patria nos espera
Impaciente; que él nos trae,
Impregnado de ternuras
Un amoroso mensaje
De aquella tierra querida
De los verdes magueyales
Y las blancas azucenas
Y los rojos tulipanes,
Nos habla de las chinampas
Florecidas; de los grandes
Centinelas que dominan
Con sus cúspides el Valle;
Y de los bellos crepúsculos
Que se bañan en la sangre

Del Sol; y de aquellas noches
De plenilunio, imborrables.
El ternísimo monólogo
Nos ha llevado un instante
En las alas del Ensueño
Hacia la Patria adorable.

Y viene el danzón Cubano.
(creación de Nelly Fernández
Y Rafael Díaz). Los dos
Nos revelan en sus bailes
Una elegancia exquisita.
Y una técnica admirable.
En el "Fox trot", surge Nelly
Bellísima, deslumbrante
Ciñendo las ricas sedas
Sus formas esculturales
Que irradian Luz y Armonía,
Juventud, Belleza y Arte.

Complementan el conjunto
Cuatro parejas de baile
Graciosas mexicanitas:
Pie pequeño y alma grande
Ojos negros de obsidiana
Y labios como corales.
Cuatro jóvenes donceles
De aquellos que avientan "piales"
Forman con ellas el coro:
Un casi coro de ángeles...

Decoraciones muy bellas
De encantadores paisajes:
Chapultepec, Xochimilco,
"El Desierto", "Los Volcanes"...

Vayan estas pobres líneas
Como rendido homenaje
De admiración y cariño
A los artistas geniales,
Que laboran por la Raza,
Por la Patria y por el Arte.

Julio de 1923
Los Angeles, Calif.

Míster BLIND

Index

Índice